Y0-AQP-574

FIELD GENERALS
MONTANA ★ WHITE
★ THEISMANN ★
ANDERSON ★

FIELD GENERALS

MONTANA ★ WHITE
★ THEISMANN ★
★ ANDERSON ★

BILL GUTMAN

ACE TEMPO BOOKS, NEW YORK

Acknowledgements

The author would like to thank the following people for providing background material and information helpful in the preparation of this book: Joe Browne, Susan McCann and their staff at National Football League headquarters; the Sports Information Departments at Augustana College, Arizona State University, and Notre Dame, Allan Heim of the Cincinnati Bengals, Joe Blair of the Washington Redskins, George Heddleston of the San Francisco 49ers, and Doug Todd of the Dallas Cowboys.

FIELD GENERALS: MONTANA, WHITE,
THEISMANN, ANDERSON

Copyright © 1982 by Bill Gutman
All rights reserved.

ISBN: 0-448-13773-9

An Ace Tempo Books Original

First Ace Tempo Printing: September 1982
Second Printing: September 1982

Tempo Books is registered in the U.S. Patent Office
Published simultaneously in Canada

Cover photos by Mickey Palmer/Focus on Sports

Manufactured in the United States of America

CONTENTS

FIELD GENERALS

MONTANA ★ WHITE
★ THEISMANN ★
★ ANDERSON ★

JOE MONTANA

When Joe Montana reported for his first varsity season at Notre Dame in 1975, he was listed as the tenth quarterback on the team's depth chart. When he completed the 1981 football season, he was named the Most Valuable Player in the Super Bowl. If one looked at these facts and guessed that quite a few things have happened to Joe Montana between 1975 and 1981, well, he'd be right.

On the surface, the blond-haired, 6-2, 200-lb. quarterback of the World Champion San Francisco 49ers seems to be living a fairy tale, a rags-to-riches story that used to only happen in the movies. But there's a lot more to it than that, and most of it can be spelled out in four words—hard work and perseverance.

Within that context, there are several separate and distinct rags-to-riches stories involving Joe Montana. Or, to be more accurate, a number of career crises where Joe had to overcome real or assumed obstacles, and prove himself all over again. He also had to overcome a very serious injury to his throwing shoulder, the breakup of an early marriage, and the opinion that he might not be first-class pro material.

But Joe Montana knew how to battle back. He had a desire deep within himself to be the best, and he learned early on to keep a cool head and play with poise no matter how difficult the situation. Those are the things champions are made of.

Joe Montana's football career has come full cycle. From a nervous high school quarterback who once lined up for the snap behind the guard instead of the center, to a college quarterback with a reputation for doing the job in relief, but bungling it as a starter, to a pro signal-caller with a supposedly suspect arm and tendency toward inconsistency, he has repeatedly risen to the top.

For instance, in 1981, he became the first NFL quarterback to lead the league in completion percentage two years in a row since 1970. He has never had the young quarterback's tendency to throw more interceptions than touchdowns. To get his team to the Super Bowl he threw the winning pass while scrambling, moving backward, leaning on the wrong foot, and with a 6'-9", All-Pro lineman practically in his face. You've got to be something special to do that.

Then there is the element of luck. Here's a perfect example. When Joe was drafted by the 49ers he was joining a team that had just completed a horrendous 2–14, season. Bad luck, right? In his rookie year of 1979, the club duplicated that 2–14 record. More bad luck, right? Wrong! For as a rookie, Joe would be working directly with the team's new coach, Bill Walsh, untested as a head coach in 1979, but reputed to be the absolute best developer of quarterbacks in the business. Two of his previous "students" were Ken Anderson of the Cincinnati Bengals and Dan Fouts of the San Diego Chargers. So the seemingly bad luck of the draft turned into a stroke of good fortune. If anyone could bring out Joe's talents quickly, it was Bill Walsh. And when he proved he could also rebuild a football team, bringing together that rapidly developing young quarterback and the rapidly improving young team, well, the rest, as they say, is history.

To trace the road that Joe Montana traveled to Super Bowl glory, it's necessary to go back to the little town of Monongahela, Pennsylvania, where Joe was born on June 11, 1956. His father was business manager for a finance company and his mother, a secretary. Joe was an only child.

Like so many future pros, Joe took to sports early, probably with some encouragement from his father. But Mr. Montana never pushed his son.

"My dad has always been a real sports lover," Joe said. "But he never tried to rush me into any sport. He just gave me one piece of advice. He said that whatever I do, I should want to be the best."

Joe played on his first football team when he was about eight. He also played baseball and basketball, and probably developed fastest as a basketball player. In fact, for awhile it was his favorite. But it wasn't long before he had a gridiron idol, and a rather exciting one at that. He was Joe Namath, who was beginning his meteoric career with the New York Jets just about the time Joe Montana was putting on shoulder pads for the first time.

There was a good reason for little Joe idolizing big Joe. Namath, of course, was a great passing quarterback, but he also grew up in Beaver Falls, Pennsylvania, which was about an hour's drive from Monongahela. So it was easy for the young boy to identify with Joe Willie. If one guy from a small Pennsylvania town could make it, why not another?

As Joe reached high school age it was still a tossup between basketball and football. At Ringgold High, he excelled at both sports and was probably noticed more as a basketball player. He used to keep an eight-foot-high hoop at his house "for dunking purposes" and play pickup games on the regulation ten-foot basket at the end of his street.

By the time he was a senior he was being recruited for

both sports. In fact, he was invited to play in the Dapper Dan Classic, an all-star basketball game in which only the top high school players participate as a showcase for college coaches. But Joe was also a fine quarterback by then, big and quick, and with a fine arm. He could later admit that he had had a certain dream for quite some time.

"I had always dreamed of playing quarterback for Notre Dame," he said. "It was something I had thought about as long as I could remember."

So in early 1974 he began sorting out the many offers that were coming his way. By then, he had just about decided that he wouldn't go to college to play basketball, so the many hoop offers he received were discarded immediately. Then there were also a good number of football offers to deal with.

"Though I knew I wanted to go to Notre Dame I wasn't sure they wanted me," Joe said. "I also wasn't sure I could make it academically. I was between a C and B student and they had high standards. There were a lot of other schools putting pressure on me then, but Notre Dame never did. I later learned they don't put pressure on any of their prospects, and that was another reason I wanted to go there. But I just didn't know how they felt right up to the time they sent me a scholarship offer. Right away I said, yes."

So it was off to South Bend, Indiana, in the fall of 1974. Whether Joe knew it or not, he was headed into a pressure cooker. The Fighting Irish had a long and marvelous football tradition, dating back to the legendary Knute Rockne and George Gipp. The school always played a top-flight schedule and the pressure to win was twofold. First of all, the alumni almost demanded it. A lot of people became very restless when the Irish weren't near or at the top. Then there was the self-induced pressure. The young players knew the tradition behind them. They wanted to uphold it.

There was also a special kind of pressure on the Notre Dame quarterback. There had been so many great ones in the past, the likes of Harry Stuhldreher, who ran the famous Four Horsemen backfield; Johnny Lujack, Angelo Bertelli, and Paul Hornung, all of whom won the Heisman Trophy; and more recent stars like Darryl Lamonica, John Huarte, Terry Hanratty, and Joe Theismann.

"Tradition plays a big part here," Joe said, after he had been at Notre Dame several years. "It comes up a lot and it's not any cornball stuff. You just don't want to let a lot of people down, because it means so much to so many to uphold the tradition. Everyone is aware of it and when things begin to go bad a bit you hear about it a little more."

Paul Hornung, who won the Heisman at Notre Dame in 1956 before going on to a Hall of Fame career with the Green Bay Packers, said things were not much different when he played.

"As far as I'm concerned it's the only place to be if you're a quarterback," Hornung said. "It's the only school in the world where I could have won the Heisman Trophy with a team that went 2–8. It's just the school's name and the so-called Subway Alumni that makes things happen. You won't find anybody in Oregon, for example, who roots for Kentucky or Miami. But you have Notre Dame fans in every state in the country."

Hornung, of course, was slightly prejudiced for his old school, but there was a great deal of truth in what he said. But Joe felt he was ready to handle the pressure and whatever else might come his way. He found the pressure, but not immediate success. As a member of the freshman team in 1974, he was the sixth of seven frosh quarterbacks, and didn't get to play that much. At this point his prospects didn't seem overwhelming.

During the offseason he returned home and married his high school sweetheart. So when he returned for his sophomore year of 1975, he was a married man and more determined than ever to make the varsity.

The starting quarterback in 1975 was Rick Slager, who was an adequate passer at best, certainly not among the top QBs of the past. At the outset of practice Joe was listed as the tenth quarterback on the depth chart. The Irish were always well stocked with players. But he worked hard all during practice, and by the time the season was set to open, he had worked himself to the point where he was the probable backup to Slager.

It promised to be a year of transition at Notre Dame. The Irish had a new coach in 1975, Dan Devine, who had been a very successful college coach, notably at Missouri, before arriving at South Bend. But Devine had also had a couple of disastrous seasons in the NFL, when he was expected to revive the glory days at Green Bay where the measuring stick was the legendary Vince Lombardi.

Now, back at Notre Dame, Devine was trying to replace another legend, Ara Parseghian. So there was a great deal of pressure on the coach as well as his players. The team was relatively inexperienced, but had the usual mammoth interior lines and good linebackers. Offensively, there were a couple of fine young running backs in Al Hunter and Jerome Heavens and an outstanding tight end in Ken MacAfee.

With Slager at the helm the Irish opened with victories over Boston College and Purdue. Then in game three with Northwestern, Slager was hurt and Joe Montana got the call for the first time. He played well and, while Northwestern didn't have a very strong team, he nevertheless led the way to a 31–7 victory. With Slager still slightly hurt, Joe got the call the following week against Michigan State.

This time it didn't go well. Joe seemed unsure and tentative, missing his targets and not making the big plays. The Spartans won the game, 10–3, to knock the

Irish from the ranks of the unbeaten. When the Irish traveled to North Carolina the following week, Rick Slager was back at the helm.

The Irish were favorites in this one, but they weren't playing well, trailing most of the way. Finally, with the club still behind, 14–7, and just six minutes left in the game, Joe once again got the call. As he trotted onto the field with the offense that day, Joe had no way of knowing that this game would mark the beginning of his own legend.

Joe knew he had to strike fast. So he threw some bombs, in between mixing the plays to his runners. In those final six minutes the Irish seemed like a different team. They rolled for two touchdowns as Joe hit on three of four passes for a whopping 129 yards. The Irish won the game, 21–14, and Joe Montana was the toast of the town.

A week later he did it again. Slager started against the Air Force Academy, and by the time Joe got the call, the Irish were behind by twenty points, 30–10. Once again he went to work, looking more like a seasoned veteran than a basically untried sophomore. Three times he marched the Irish in for scores, hitting seven passes for 134 yards and two touchdowns. Notre Dame won the game, 31–30, with Joe as the miracle worker. Immediately people were calling him the Comeback Kid, a guy who could pull it off in the final minutes. The question now was, could he do it going all the way?

He started the next game, the traditional battle with Southern Cal, and again he faltered. The Trojans won, 24–17, with Joe seeming to lack that electricity he brought with him when he entered late in the game. There were those who said he could come in and give a team an immediate lift, but he couldn't seem to handle a club all the way, execute a game plan calmly and efficiently.

The situation also caused Dan Devine to keep

switching his quarterbacks. Without a firm number one, the entire team was undoubtedly hurt, because there is often a change in rhythm with a change of quarterbacks. In addition, the constant switching failed to help either of the two players.

"Rick and I were good friends," Joe recalled, "and we used to talk about the pressure that was on us. What happened was that we were both scared half the time we were out there. We both felt that if we made just one mistake we'd be pulled out and the other guy would come in. So we'd constantly be looking over our shoulders at the coach to make sure he wasn't ready to yank us out. Because of this, neither one really felt the confidence that you need to be number one."

Perhaps this feeling also explains why Joe played so well with the game on the line. He was aware that he was being sent out to try to win the game and he could pull out all the stops without worrying. If he failed, well, he was sent into tough situations, anyway, and there wasn't time to think about mistakes. On the other hand, when he was starting, that same late-game frenzy wasn't there. He had to think about executing the routine plays, the automatic ones. If things went sour then, there was ample time for a change, and the coaches would make one.

The problem was resolved in the next game against Navy. Joe started and now was playing fairly well. Of course, the Midshipmen had a weaker team, but maybe it was what he needed. What he didn't need was an injury to his throwing hand. It caused him to give way to Slager, and it would also cause him to miss the final three games. Slager finished up as the Irish won two of the final three to complete the season at 8–3. Not bad, but certainly not good enough for Notre Dame.

Joe threw just 66 passes as a sophomore in 1975, completing 28 for 507 yards and four scores. However, he was intercepted eight times and had a completion percentage of just 42.4. By contrast, Slager completed 66 of 139, but for just 686 yards and two scores. Still, Joe knew there was room for a great deal of improvement. There was no way he could complete barely more than forty percent of his passes and be a successful quarterback at Notre Dame.

So he looked forward to 1976. When it came time for spring practice he was ready to go. Rick Slager would be back, and Joe was hoping to get a leg up on the starting job. He preferred not to be shuttled in and out as he was the past season. Then one day he was working against the first team defense, which was getting ready to work on their goal-line stand.

"I was supposed to throw a little fake for a play-action pass," he said. "I started the fake and my feet got caught on turf. As I stumbled, one of our defensive ends, Willy Fry, who weighed about 240, hit me a good shot and I went down hard on my right shoulder. The pain told me right away that it was bad. It's funny. I'd never been seriously hurt in a ball game before, but as soon as it happened, I knew this one was serious."

It was about as serious an injury that a quarterback could get. Joe's right shoulder was separated and whenever there's an injury to the throwing arm, the nagging questions arise. Will it heal completely? Will my arm be as strong as it was before? Will the shoulder be more susceptible to separating again?

Joe had to be thinking about these things, especially when they put him in a cast from his hip to his shoulder. The cast didn't stay on long, but when it came off, the doctors told Joe to use his arm as little as possible. Joe knew that he had a decision to make.

"It became obvious that I wouldn't be ready, mentally or physically, by the time the 1976 season started," he explained. "I could have been with the squad and sat on the bench. But I had always wanted to take a shot at pro ball, to see if I could cut it. If I sat on the bench as a junior another quarterback might establish himself and I wouldn't play much my senior year. If that happened, I knew I wouldn't be drafted. So I decided to redshirt the '76 season. That way, I'd still have two years of eligibility left."

Redshirting isn't easy, not for a guy who had never been hurt before and who had been playing football every autumn for nearly a dozen years. In short, it was a depressing experience. Quarterbacks are usually in the forefront of everything and among the most recognizable players on a team. To suddenly be pushed into the background, out of the spotlight, had to make Joe wonder what the future would bring.

The team had another 8–3 season without Joe. Rick Slager was the quarterback again and a pair of youngsters, Rusty Lisch and Gary Forystek, were working behind him. Both would be back and competing with Joe the next year. So sitting out was somewhat of a gamble and Joe knew it.

Fortunately, when 1977 rolled around Joe's shoulder had healed and he was showing no ill effects from the injury. But he was competing for the job with Lisch and Forystek, just as he had anticipated, and in the early going it looked as if Lisch had the inside track. Having sat out the entire season before, Joe knew he'd have to win the job back on the field. He only hoped that he would get the chance.

The Irish had a big, tough team in 1977. The principal worry was that they might be too slow. In addition, there was talk about whether any of the quarterbacks would really be able to move the club. Then, as expected, Coach Devine named Rusty Lisch as the starter in the opening game at Pittsburgh. Lisch went all the way as the Irish won, 19–9. But much of the credit for the victory had to go to the defense, which forced six Panther turnovers in the final period alone. The offense looked sluggish.

Joe was chomping at the bit as he sat on the bench that day. It bothered him, for several reasons.

"It really hurt me not getting in that first game," he said, "especially since we were playing so close to my home town. My folks and a lot of my friends had come to see me. No one likes sitting on the bench. You want to play, but you realize that a coach can play only eleven men at a time and he has to pick the ones he thinks are best. Still, realizing that doesn't help when you've always been accustomed to playing, to being a starter and a star. I knew Rusty was a good quarterback, but naturally you wouldn't be much of a player if you didn't think you could do better."

There were even rumors around then that Joe and Coach Devine weren't on the best of terms. That might have been true to some extent, but Devine was too much of a professional to let personal feelings cloud his judgement when the good of his football team was at stake.

Yet Lisch went all the way again the next week, and this time it was obvious the offense just wasn't responding. The Irish were upset by a mediocre Mississippi team, 20–13, and Joe began to really wonder if he would get a chance. The following week the Irish would be playing their third straight road game, this one at Purdue, and the Boilermakers always seemed to give Notre Dame a tough time.

But when game time rolled around, Lisch was back at the helm with Joe sinking further into the bench. Again the Irish offense seemed to lack spark. The club had a solid running game with Jerome Heavens and Vagas Ferguson, and an all-American tight end in Ken MacAfee, but they just weren't sustaining any kind of attack.

"I was sure the coach was going to put me in the game," Joe said, as the Irish began falling behind.

Finally, late in the second period Devine made a

change. But it was Gary Forystek who got the call and
Joe was really thinking doom and gloom.

"I really felt shot down," he recalled. "I thought I was
the number two quarterback and then there was Gary
going into the game."

But Forystek didn't last long. On his first series of
plays a Purdue linebacker put a shot on him and he
stayed down. When he was helped from the field it was
quickly determined that his collarbone was broken.
Now Joe had to get the call. Wrong. Devine returned
Lisch to the game.

"Then I wasn't sure if I'd ever get a chance to play,"
said Joe.

It was more of the same with Lisch back, and by late
in the third period the Irish were behind by a 24–14
count. Then, at long last, the coach told Joe to warm up.
He was going in on the next series of plays. There he was,
in the game before some 70,000 fans, most of them rooting for the Boilermakers.

"I was really scared," he admitted. "I didn't know
how I'd react to the pressure. After all, I hadn't thrown
a pass in a real game in nearly two years. I didn't want
the other guys to know how I felt, so I called a short pass
to MacAfee, a relatively simple play I thought would
give me a feel for the action. I remember the pass float-
ing end over end, way short, and almost being intercepted."

It took a few minutes and a couple of hits from the
Purdue defense, but by the fourth quarter the ner-
vousness was gone and Joe was feeling more like his own
self. He took a deep breath and went to work. Suddenly,
it was 1975 again and Joe Montana was picking apart
the Purdue defense.

He did the job long and short, and once he began
finding his receivers, the Irish backs began slashing
through suddenly wider holes. The final period belonged
to Notre Dame and to Joe Montana. He completed nine

of 14 passes for 154 yards in just sixteen minutes of action, as the Irish rallied for seventeen, fourth-quarter points to win the game. For his efforts, Joe was named UPI Midwest Back of the Week, and he was also named the starting quarterback for the following week against Michigan State.

It was what he had wanted, yet in the week preceding the game with the Spartans, Joe was visibly nervous. He remembered all those stories in 1975, that he was great coming off the bench in desperate, no-holds-barred situations, but he couldn't cut it as a starter. So he still had plenty left to prove.

"I was very shaky when I went out there against Michigan State," he said. "Part of the reason was that my first start in 1975 had been against Michigan State and I just didn't execute well and we lost the game. I just kind of had a vision of it all happening again."

Joe didn't set the world on fire that day. But he and his teammates played well enough to win, 16–6. They beat Army the next week, 24–0, further establishing Joe as the number one quarterback. Then they had to prepare for the big one; playing host to USC, then ranked number two in the nation.

The afternoon started on an emotional high when the Irish came out of their locker room in bright green jerseys, the first time they had donned those threads since 1963, and it threw the crowd into an immediate frenzy. From there, Joe and his offense took over. They ripped through the strong USC defense all afternoon, and when it was over they had buried the Trojans, 49–19.

It was a glorious day for Joe, his best since coming to Notre Dame. He completed 13 of 24 passes for 167 yards and two scores. MacAfee was on the receiving end of eight of his aerials, while Joe himself scored two times on the ground. The win boosted the Irish into the national rankings and firmly established Joe Montana as the number one quarterback.

"You could say that game was the turning point of the season for us," Joe said. "After Southern Cal, we knew we could play with anybody."

It also seemed to give Joe the final shot of confidence he needed. In big wins over Navy and Georgia Tech the following two weeks he threw for more than 260 yards in each game. It was the first time a Notre Dame quarterback had thrown for that much yardage in successive games since the days of Joe Theismann in 1970. Against Clemson a week later he scored two, fourth-quarter touchdowns to bring the Irish from behind once more, 21–17. Victories over the Air Force, 49–0, Miami, 48–10, closed out the season with the Irish seeming to get stronger and stronger, especially offensively.

The club was 10–1 for the year and ranked fourth nationally. Now they had a New Year's Day date in the Cotton Bowl against mighty Texas, unbeaten at 11–0, ranked number one in the nation, and led by the best running back in the land, Heisman Trophy winner Earl Campbell. The Irish would be decided underdogs.

Joe's stats for the regular season were very impressive. In nine games he had completed 99 of 189 passes for 1,604 yards and eleven touchdowns. His completion percentage was up to 52.4, he threw just eight intercepts, and scored another six touchdowns on the ground.

He had fine support from Heavens, who ran for 994 yards, and Ferguson, who gained 493. MacAfee led the receivers with 54 catches for 797 yards and six scores. All-Americans Bob Golic and Ross Browner were the leading defenders. During the season the Irish outscored their opponents, 382 to 129. So it was indeed a powerful Notre Dame team that came out to meet Texas in the Cotton Bowl. The majority of fans in the Dallas Stadium were there to root the Longhorns to a national title. But that didn't bother the Irish in the least.

They dominated the game from the opening kickoff. Both their offensive and defensive lines manhandled the smaller Longhorns, and never allowed them to use their speed to any real advantage. The defense also controlled the great Earl Campbell, while Joe picked apart the Texas secondary with his fine passing. He also executed beautifully and the Irish made it look easy. They won it, 38–10.

But that wasn't the most exciting part. Going in, the Irish were ranked fourth. They not only wiped out the nation's number one team, but the clubs ranked two and three also lost in Bowl game upsets. So when the final AP and UPI polls were counted, Notre Dame had won the national championship.

It was a wild time at the South Bend campus. After splitting their first two games and not looking anything like a team contending for national honors, the Irish had come on like gangbusters, getting better and better as the season wore on. In their final six games of the regular season the offense scored 49, 43, 69, 21, 49, and 48 points. Then they got thirty-eight against powerful Texas.

A big part of the transformation had to be the elevation of Joe Montana to the number one quarterback slot. Joe had finally proved he could do more than bail the team out in the closing minutes. Surrounded by an outstanding cast, Joe did the job to the tune of being named honorable mention all-America. It looked as if he had made the right decision when he redshirted in 1976. Now he had still another season of eligibility and many were predicting that he could be the premier college quarterback in the country in 1978. His prospects of going high in the pro draft were definitely improved.

Yet there was one development during the off-season. Joe and his wife had separated. Friends, of course, hoped the couple would get back together and Coach Devine hoped Joe's personal problems wouldn't affect his performance on the field. The Irish had a tougher schedule in '78, and as defending national champs, everyone would be gunning for them.

In addition, the club graduated four genuine all-Americans in tight end MacAfee, defensive end Ross Browner, defensive back Luther Bradley, and center Ernie Hughes. So each unit was hit with a big loss. Then came the first two games and disaster. The team blew one opportunity after another and lost its opener to Missouri, 3–0. A week later they got a lead on Michigan and couldn't hold it, losing 28–14. So the mighty Irish, defending national champs, were at 0–2, and already people were screaming for a coaching change. The quarterback wasn't about to be changed, but Joe wasn't playing well, either.

He had been intercepted four times in the first two games and the Irish as a team had ten turnovers.

"People were not only getting on Coach Devine, but on everyone, including me," Joe said. "Aside from the turnovers it's possible we may have been resting on last year's laurels. In fact, the hardest part is trying to get people to forget about last year. The national championship means tremendous personal satisfaction, but that was last year. We've got to get it together again now."

The team played better the next week, beating Purdue, 10–6, though Joe had two more intercepts. But Vagas Ferguson was emerging as a genuine all-American candidate at halfback, and teamed with Jerome Heavens the Irish had a very solid one-two running punch. What Joe lacked was an outstanding single receiver, the role MacAfee had filled the year before. So he had to spread things out somewhat.

After the Purdue game the Irish seemed to be improving. They whipped Michigan State, 29–25, then faced unbeaten Pittsburgh. And once again Joe Montana slipped into the uniform of the Comeback Kid. The Panthers had a 17–7 lead going into the final period.

But the Comeback Kid came out throwing. Joe had

the magic again and he completed his last seven consecutive passes for 110 yards. His hot streak enabled the Irish to score 19 fourth-period points and win the game, 26–17. Once more his clutch performance drew headlines, plus the usual review of his last-second victories in the past.

"I keep thinking Joe Montana's been at Notre Dame for something like eight years," kidded Joe Theismann, the Irish quarterback in the late 1960s and in 1970, and now the starter for the Washington Redskins. "It just seems that Joe has run that team longer than the rest of us. Seems like every year you keep reading about him pulling out ballgames."

Joe Montana knew exactly what Theismann meant. There was an awful lot of exposure at Notre Dame and it probably made some people feel he had been there forever.

"The exposure here is tremendous," he said. "But so is the pressure to perform. There are probably many more people watching what I do each week, and what the team does, than with most other schools."

What the team was doing was embarking on an eight-game winning streak. Running back Ferguson was headed for a 1,000-yard season and Joe had stopped throwing the intercepts and was now running the offense with cool efficiency. After Pittsburgh, the Air Force fell, soon followed by Miami, Navy, Tennessee, and Georgia Tech. The club had rebounded to 8–2. They would close the season by traveling to the Los Angeles Coliseum to meet the always powerful Trojans of Southern California, coming in with a 9–1 mark.

USC had a great defense in '78, having allowed just 113 points in ten games prior to the Irish, and they hadn't allowed more than two touchdowns in any one game.

"It's a typical USC team," said Joe. "They're relatively big and fast, and do so many things much like a pro team. They always have very good athletes, so it doesn't really matter how young they are."

As expected, the game produced more than its share of excitement. Both teams were sky-high and the outcome could go a long way in determining the final rankings. The national title might not be at stake, but you wouldn't know it by the way both teams played. Unfortunately, for the Irish, it was the Trojans who did most of the damage for three periods. Though the Irish were playing well, they weren't making the big plays and they trailed badly.

Then came the fourth quarter, and in his final regular season game, Joe brought out the Comeback Kid once more. By now it was as if everyone expected it, so when he began connecting with his receivers, it was almost routine, though a pretty exciting routine.

During the final session, Joe threw for two touchdowns and set up a third, putting the Irish ahead, 25–24. It looked like another of his patented finishes. But the Trojans had one final chance. And they wouldn't quit, either. They moved into Irish territory, and with just seconds remaining, Frank Jordan booted a long field goal to win the game for USC, 27–25. It was a tough loss, but Joe felt his club could hold its head high.

"We could have been blown out if we had given up," he said. "But we didn't. We came back fighting and that's the important thing. And I don't deserve all the credit for the comeback. I had a great offense around me and our defense always has to get us the ball."

The loss to Southern Cal gave the Irish a final mark of 8–3, and made a Cotton Bowl date with Houston a lot less meaningful. Only in that game, Joe Montana gave Notre Dame fans one final look at the Comeback Kid.

The Cougars were a 9–2 team coming in with a very strong defense against the run. They also had a fine offense and showed both traits in running up a 34–12 lead, which they held midway into the final period. It seemed

like too big a margin for Joe to make up. But he took a
deep breath and went to work anyway.

Once again he seemed to instill his magic into the entire Notre Dame team. He marched his team down the
field three times in those final minutes, scoring the final
touchdown himself with no time left on the clock. Then
he calmly threw for a two-point conversion to win the
game, 35–34. It might have been his greatest miracle finish of all. He completed 13 passes for 163 yards and one
touchdown. Plus he ran for 34 yards and scored twice
himself. In addition to that, he also threw for two clutch,
two-point conversions. It was one heckava way to end a
college career.

During the regular season of 1978, Joe completed 141
of 260 passes for 2,010 yards, a 54.2 percentage, and ten
touchdowns. He had just nine intercepted. His career
log read 290 of 515 for 4,121 yards, a 52.2 percentage,
and 25 scores. The kid from Monongahela, who wasn't
sure Notre Dame wanted him, football wise or
academically, graduated as an all-American and with a
Bachelor's Degree in Marketing.

But the only thing he wanted to market then was his
right arm and his ability to lead a football team. He
admitted again before the Cotton Bowl game with
Houston that he really wanted to play pro ball.

"It's something I've always dreamed of doing," he
said. "Now that it's here and I'm so close to it, I'd like
to give it a try."

With all his credentials—quarterbacking Notre Dame
to a national title and two other winning seasons, his
stats, and that incredible ability to pull a game out—it
seemed that Joe might very well be a first round draft
choice, perhaps quite near the top of the heap. But the
NFL scouting reports dictated otherwise. Joe did not get
top grades in all categories. The scouts seemed to think
he was inconsistent, perhaps judging from the six intercepts he threw in the first three games of '78. Or

perhaps it was the old story about him performing miracles with the game on the line, but often having troubles early in the contest running the regular game plan. There were also questions about his arm. They said he didn't throw long very often at Notre Dame, and was more of a "touch" passer. Many NFL coaches like their quarterbacks to have a gun for an arm.

For these reasons, Joe was bypassed in the first round of the draft. Then the second round came . . . and went. Still no takers. It was strongly reminiscent of what happened with another former Notre Dame quarterback, Joe Theismann. He was a consensus all-America and almost won the Heisman Trophy, yet wasn't taken until the third round because the scouts thought he was too small. It took awhile, but Theismann proved them wrong.

It looked as if Montana would have to do the same thing. Like Theismann, he finally got the call on the third round. But unlike Theismann, who was picked by a top team, Joe Montana was headed for the bottom. He was the third round pick of the San Francisco 49ers, a club that had finished the 1978 season with an inglorious record of two victories and fourteen defeats!

In fact, the 49ers had fallen on hard times. The club had never won a championship, to begin with, and that streak had reached more than thirty years duration, since 1946, longest of any pro-football team. They had become a playoff club in the early 1970s, but were always eliminated before reaching the conference championship or Super Bowl.

Then in the mid to late 1970s, a series of bad deals and poor draft selections had caused the team to bottom out. One perfect example. The 49ers had acquired the great O.J. Simpson from Buffalo so that O.J. could finish his career in his hometown, and hopefully inject some magic into the 49ers offense. But this proved wrong as the Juice was coming off knee surgery and was just a shell of his former self. He hardly helped the club at all, except perhaps to draw a few more fans through the turnstiles. For this, the club lost several top draft choices.

The club did rebound in 1976 to an 8–6 record, but then the ownership changed hands and new coaches came in again. The club dipped to 5–9 in '77, and then dropped all the way to 2–14 the following year. That's when the new owners hired Bill Walsh to help turn the club around. As he had done in his stops at Cincinnati and San Diego, as well as in his stint as head coach at Stanford, Walsh planned to build around a diverse and devastating passing attack. He had been refining his offensive theories over the years and felt he was ready to be an NFL head man. He also knew he would need a special kind of quarterback to run his attack. As mentioned earlier, Bill Walsh was the man who developed both Ken Anderson and Dan Fouts, so there was no doubt about the coach's ability in that area.

The incumbent quarterbacks when Walsh took over were both unproven youngsters, Steve DeBerg and Scott Bull. DeBerg had seen most of the action in 1978 and was near the bottom of the quarterback rankings. Walsh thought he had possibilities, but there was another problem.

"We didn't really have a healthy quarterback," the new coach said. "Both DeBerg and Bull were coming off knee surgery so we knew we would have to draft a quarterback because we couldn't go into the season having two quarterbacks with questionable knees."

The day before the draft, the 49ers had several college quarterbacks work out for the coaches. Among them were Steve Dils, whom Walsh had coached at Stanford, and Joe Montana. Walsh, of course, knew what the scouting reports had said about Joe, but he wanted to see for himself.

"He showed us he was pretty sound," the coach said, "and we already knew of his resourcefulness because of what he did at Notre Dame. Another thing I noticed was that he was very quick afoot, and I liked that."

So it was Montana whom the 49ers made their choice. Perhaps Joe was disappointed because he didn't go higher, but he knew of Walsh's reputation with quarterbacks and figured the 49ers could go no place but up. In addition, he liked the Bay Area, so it wasn't really a bad situation for him.

The 49ers still had plenty of holes to fill in 1979. It was not the kind of situation in which to throw a rookie quarterback. DeBerg had the most experience and Walsh decided he would be the man to run the offense. Joe would be brought along slowly.

That's exactly what happened in 1979. Walsh felt the 49ers could be contenders within two years, meaning 1981, but judging by 1979, not too many people believed him. The club duplicated its 2–14 record of a year earlier. But there were some differences. The 49ers became the passingest team in the league. Steve DeBerg went virtually all the way and set an NFL record for completions, though many of them were short passes, dumpoffs in NFL terms.

Still, Walsh was developing a passing attack that moved the ball. The problem was still a porous defense that almost anyone could march through. The Niners gave up a total of 416 points in sixteen games.

As expected, Joe was brought along slowly. Though Walsh and the coaches worked extensively with him in practice and in skull sessions, allowing him to absorb the coach's concepts, he saw virtually no action on the field. His main action came as the holder for placekicker Ray Wersching. Joe threw just two passes in his first eleven NFL games. He was one out of one against L.A. for eight yards, and one of one against Atlanta for minus eight. So his net gain was zero.

Then in game twelve against Denver he got in long enough to complete three of five in the NFL. Finally, in the fourteenth game of the year, he got a start at St. Louis, though he didn't do anything spectacular. Yet he kept his mistakes to a minimum.

When the season ended, Joe had thrown 23 passes, completing 13 for 96 yards and one touchdown. Not even a good day's work. But Joe didn't expect too much more, so he wasn't really disappointed. He was looking forward to 1980, though he didn't want to sit all the way again.

The club made some improvements in 1980. They drafted a big fullback out of Rice, Earl Cooper, who could catch the ball as well as run it. If halfback Paul Hofer stayed healthy he, too, was a fine receiver, as well as runner. Walsh's backs had to catch.

His outside receivers were also improving. Freddie Solomon had come over from Miami and was a speedy gamebreaker. Young Dwight Clark was a fine pattern runner and improving each year. Walsh then acquired former all-pro tight end Charlie Young, who was wasting away on the Los Angeles Rams bench. The problem again would be the defense, which had a combination of youngsters, veterans, and journeymen players.

DeBerg got the call in the opener against the New Orleans Saints and he played very well, leading the 49ers to a 26–23 victory. The club certainly didn't appear like a 2–14 team any more. DeBerg completed 21 of 29 passes for 223 yards. Again he was throwing mainly to his backs. Hofer caught seven for 114 yards and rookie Cooper grabbed 10 for 71 yards. But DeBerg was executing the game plan and if he continued to produce, Joe might find himself doing more sitting than he bargained for.

A week later they did it again, beating St. Louis, 24–21, in overtime. Once again DeBerg looked sharp, with 25 of 42 for 266 yards and a pair of scores. The club also ran for 132 yards, so they had some balance. The one negative part of DeBerg's game was his three interceptions. He had four in two games, though he was completing almost 65 percent of his passes.

Then in game three with the New York Jets, a very significant thing happened. Bill Walsh began working Joe Montana into the lineup. DeBerg started as usual, and early in the first period drove the club downfield, then tossed a 15-yard TD pass to Charlie Young. Wersching's kick made it 7–0. Later in the period the club marched down to the Jets' 5. Suddenly, DeBerg was coming out and number 16, Joe Montana, came in.

DeBerg had a bad throat and had been using special equipment to amplify his voice. At first it was thought he left for an equipment repair. Not so.

"It was prearranged that I would fake a problem with the equipment," DeBerg said. "Coach Walsh wanted to get Joe in the game, because he's a lot quicker than I am."

The play was bootleg, and Joe ran it perfectly, taking it into the end zone for another score. The fact that Walsh was taking advantage of his quickness, those fast feet he had talked about, might have been a foreshadowing. Despite his passing success, Steve DeBerg was basically a very immobile quarterback.

In the second period they did the same thing. The ball was on the New York 20 when DeBerg came out. Joe came on again and promptly threw a 20-yard TD pass to Dwight Clark. The two had devised the play on the sideline and Walsh wanted to give it a try. The Niners went on to a 24–0 lead, which became 24–3 at the half.

Then in the third period Joe got another chance, and spearheaded a drive that led to a seven-yard TD toss to Clark. DeBerg later returned and hit Freddie Solomon with a 38-yard scoring toss. Though the Jets made a comeback in the final session, the Niners won it, 37–27. The club was 3–0 and beginning to write a real Cinderella story.

DeBerg had another solid game with 17 of 23 for 180 yards, but Joe also chipped in this time, hitting four of six for sixty yards and the two touchdowns. It felt good to see some action.

The bubble burst the following week and the club lost a close 20–17 decision to the Falcons. DeBerg put the ball up all afternoon, hitting 32 of 51 passes for 345 big yards, including a 93-yard touchdown pass to Solomon. DeBerg's 32 completions set a team record, as did the 93-yard scoring toss. So there was still no clear indication that Joe Montana might take away the job. DeBerg was completing more than 65 percent of his passes and had thrown for more yardage than any other QB in the NFC.

But the next week the club was beaten badly by the Rams, as DeBerg threw two more intercepts. Then came the Dallas Cowboys and a game none of the 49ers would ever forget.

The Cowboys marched through the 49ers as if they were Pee Wee Leaguers. By halftime it was 38–7, and the final count was 59–14. It was the club's third straight loss and obviously, the worst one yet.

DeBerg had a horrendous day, completing just 12 of 35, and tossing five interceptions, giving him thirteen in six games. Word had it that Walsh was very upset with his quarterback and thought about a change to Montana the following week in the rematch with the Rams. Then, days before the game, it was confirmed. Joe would be starting against L.A.

"I've thought about it and it's scary," Joe admitted. "But if you're going to start it might as well be against the best."

It also wasn't the most pleasant situation for Joe because he and DeBerg were roommates and good friends. But he knew this was the nature of sports. Everybody wanted to start.

"It's a tough situation to be in," Joe said. "Steve had been playing well until last week. He's more of a touch thrower than I am. His ball has a tighter spiral. But they say I'm a better runner. I know we're both competitors.

"Coach Walsh has also said that he doesn't want to juggle the quarterbacks back and forth. So now I've got as much of a chance as Steve, and that's all I ask. I've wanted to start more, but I'm not the kind of guy to say 'play me or trade me.' I guess it could have come to that if I continued to sit, but not this year.

"I've been waiting for the chance and when Coach Walsh called me into his office and asked me if I was ready to start, I said yes. Last year was a big learning year for me. I knew I wasn't ready then. But I got a chance to start in the preseason this year and I'm more comfortable running the offense. I'm not nearly as nervous as I was last year."

Still, it was the kind of situation where Joe knew he had to do well. If he fell on his face, the coach could easily go back to DeBerg, and who knows when his chance would come again.

There were some 55,000 fans at Candlestick Park to watch Joe run the 49ers' offense for the first time in 1980. Neither team scored in the first period, though Joe was looking poised and unruffled in the face of the rugged Ram defense. But in the second period L.A. began taking charge. They just had too much firepower and depth for the Niners. Though a Ray Wersching field goal got San Francisco on the board first, L.A.'s Vince Ferragamo hit a pair of scoring passes to make it 14–3 at the half.

By the end of three it was 24–3. Joe managed to lead a couple of solid drives in the fourth period, throwing short scoring passes to Young and Solomon, but the Rams won easily, 31–17. Still, Joe had played well, hitting 21 of 37 passes for 252 yards and two scores. He also had a pair picked off. He didn't play the Comeback Kid, but he had held his own.

So the Niners had lost four straight, and much of the problem was still the defense. The club led the NFL by averaging 246.7 yards passing per game, and the top receivers in the league were running backs Hofer and Cooper, with forty-one and forty catches respectively. Dwight Clark was tied for fourth in the NFC with 32. But the Niners were essentially running a short passing game, as evidenced by the number of dump offs.

Joe probably wondered if Coach Walsh would go back to DeBerg against the Tampa Bay Buccaneers. He didn't. Joe was again at the helm, and this one was a real heartbreaker. A Freddie Solomon punt return and a pair of Wershing field goals gave the Niners a 13–7 lead at the half. In the third period the Bucs took a 14–13 lead, but Joe came right back with a 45-yard touchdown toss to halfback Lenvil Elliott. San Francisco led, 20–14, only to have the Bucs score again to make it 21–20 after three.

Then in the fourth period Joe went to work. He was in the midst of hitting thirteen straight passes, to set a 49ers' team record, and he drove the club eighty-one yards to the Tampa Bay 1. There they had a fourth-down play and Coach Walsh elected to go for the field goal. It was good, giving the Niners a 23–21 lead. What they didn't count on was the Bucs coming back and Garo Yepremian booting a 30-yarder with just forty-seven seconds left to pull it out, 24–23.

That made five straight losses. But Joe was starting to do things. He was 24 of 31 for 200 yards, and now he had thrown enough passes to appear in fourth place in the quarterback ratings. He was hitting more than 65 percent of his passes and had thrown for seven scores with just four intercepts. It was beginning to look as if the kid from Notre Dame might make it after all.

The next week Joe started and was six of 11 when DeBerg came in against the Lions. He finished with 15 of 31 for 146 yards as the Niners lost again, 17–13, when Charlie Young dropped a pass in the end zone. But De-Berg was at the helm again the following week as the losing streak reached seven. This time the Packers beat the Niners, 23–16, with DeBerg going 18 for 35 for 265 yards. It looked as if Walsh was shuffling his players to try to end the drought.

Loss number eight came at the hands of the Miami Dolphins, who took a hard-fought, 17–13, win. Again DeBerg went most of the way, hitting 29 of 41 for 225 yards, and along the way he hit fifteen straight, breaking the mark Joe set just a few weeks earlier. Joe did get in at the end to complete three of four. But the job once again seemed up for grabs.

Then the losing streak ended. They did it against the lowly New York Giants, with Joe starting and DeBerg pitching relief. A Montana swing pass to Earl Cooper in the second period turned into a 66-yard touchdown jaunt. Later in the same period a safety and a Wersching field goal completed the scoring. The Niners won, 12–0, but they won.

Joe was nine for 15 for 151 yards, the TD toss to Cooper, and two intercepts. DeBerg came on to go seven of 12 for 65 yards. It was still hard to tell which quarterback Walsh would finally settle with. In an article about the team in a weekly sports publication, the writer said:

"Although Joe Montana looks like an NFL quarterback, it's too early to tell."

But the next week he seemed to be reclaiming the job, leading the club over New England, 21–17, hitting 14 of 23 for 123 yards and three big touchdowns. Though he barely had enough attempts to qualify, Joe was now the second best passer in the NFC. By contrast, DeBerg had dropped to thirteenth and Joe was about to have the greatest game of his pro career.

It came against the league's weakest team, the New Orleans Saints, a club that had lost all thirteen games it had played thus far in 1980. But against the 49ers they came out like Super Bowl champs. By halftime they had a 35–7 lead, totally embarrassing Joe and the Niners. But suddenly, as the second half began, Joe seemed to turn back the clock. He was at Notre Dame again and sent in to pull out an important game.

Somewhere under that helmet and all those pads was the uniform of the Comeback Kid. It didn't take Joe long to go to work. In the third period he drove the team downfield and scored himself from the one. Later in the session he want up top and hit Dwight Clark on a 71-yard scoring bomb. That brought the score to 35–21 as the final period began.

He hit Freddie Solomon from the 14, and with time running down led another drive that resulted in Lenvil Elliott scoring from the 7 tying the game at 35–35. The Niner defense was also doing the job and the game went into sudden-death overtime.

Some seven minutes into the overtime Joe drove the Niners into New Orleans territory again, and Ray Wersching won it with a 36-yard field goal. Joe had completed 24 of 36 passes for 285 yards and two scores. He didn't have a pass picked off and his performance took him to the top of the NFC quarterback ratings and second best in the NFL. He was completing better than 64 percent of his passes, had thrown thirteen TDs and had just seven intercepted. More and more it began to look as if Joe Montana was the 49ers' quarterback.

Though the club lost its two final games to playoff-bound Atlanta and Buffalo, Joe continued to play well. The club finished at 6–10, an improvement over the 2–14 of the two previous years, and they might have found themselves a quarterback.

He finished the year completing 176 of 273 passes for an NFL best 64.5 completion percentage, gaining 1,795 yards with 15 touchdowns and nine intercepts. He eventually wound up as the fourth-best passer in the NFC. Two things stood out for a basically inexperienced signal-caller. First the high completion percentage. Young QBs often have a hard time completing fifty percent of their passes. Second was the low number of intercepts.

Young throwers usually make more mistakes.

The Niners had shown they could put points on the scoreboard, but the defense had again given up more than 400. With the offense about set, the team decided to go after defensive help, with the draft and via the free agent route. What they did has to go down as some of the more brilliant personnel moves in NFL history.

When the draft rolled around, the club wasted no time in shoring up a very porous secondary that had just one quality player, free safety Dwight Hicks. The number one pick was USC's all-American safety, Ronnie Lott, who would be converted to cornerback. The second choice was Missouri cornerback Eric Wright, and the third, strong safety Carlton Williamson of Pittsburgh. All three defied the odds by becoming starters—and stars—in their rookie season. Lott, in fact, became an all-pro.

Then there was the defensive line, lacking a good pass rush. The Niners promptly picked up Fred Dean, who was disgruntled over his contract with the Chargers. Dean was perhaps the finest pass rusher in the entire NFL, at worst among the top five. Another problem solved. The club also lacked stability at linebacker, with veteran Willie Harper perhaps the only solid performer. Once again the club picked up an unhappy veteran, middle linebacker Jack "Hacksaw" Reynolds, who had spent eleven seasons with the Rams.

"I wasn't excited when we got Reynolds," said defensive coordinator Chuck Studley. "I figured he would just occupy a spot that might be better taken by a young, developing player. But I was grossly in error. Jack became invaluable to our defense. He's the most thoroughly dedicated football player I've ever known."

So the pieces seemed to be falling into place. And what about the quarterback slot? Would the two players be sharing the position again. Not this time. Bill Walsh made sure there would be no problem. Before the season started he traded Steve DeBerg to Denver. The job belonged to Joe Montana. Then the coach made a startling admission, which probably surprised even Joe himself.

"We felt Joe was our quarterback of the future all along," he said. "By working him in the way we did last year, we gave him good exposure to the National Football League. We were criticized more than a few times for the way we handled the quarterbacks. People said that we couldn't make up our minds on a number one. But we knew that Joe was our man. It was just a matter of getting him the exposure and trying to keep winning with DeBerg at the same time."

So the coach who develops quarterbacks had his man tabbed from the outset. He also felt his team was now ready to challenge for the NFC West crown, though few so-called experts agreed. There were too many "ifs," starting with the three rookies who had all won starting berths in the defensive backfield. It takes several years for cornerbacks to mature, reasoned the experts. In addition, halfback Paul Hofer had gone down with a severe knee injury during 1980 and there was a big question as to whether he could regain his old form, if he could play at all.

No one was worried about the pass receivers. Rookie Cooper had led the NFC with eighty-three catches from his fullback position, in addition to gaining 720 yards rushing. Dwight Clark was right behind with eighty-two catches, Solomon was a legitimate deep threat, and Charlie Young could still cut it. The only question was whether Joe Montana could continue to run the offense successfully.

"Joe understands the total concept of our intricate system incredibly well for a young quarterback," said Sam Wyche, the Niners' quarterback coach. "He makes quick, intelligent decisions during a play when he has to pick and choose his receivers. He knows precisely what is right or wrong with a play as soon as it happens."

The team opened in Detroit and received a bad omen when Ray Wersching pulled a leg muscle in the warm-ups. That hurt the kicking game and gave the Lions good field position all afternoon. Yet it was a 17–17 game when Detroit made one last drive and scored the winning touchdown with just eighteen seconds left. Joe had a good opener, hitting 18 of 28 for 195 yards and a touchdown. But the club lost.

Walsh pointed to the running game. Earl Cooper had gained just twenty-two yards. Hofer was in for one play, but it still wasn't known if the knee would hold up. The coach added that he was pleased with Joe and the wide receivers.

A week later the running game improved somewhat, but it was Joe Montana who really took charge. Playing against the Chicago Bears, Joe completed 20 of 32 passes for 287 yards and three scores. Among them was a 31-yarder to halfback Ricky Patton and a 46-yarder to Solomon. The final was 28–17, as Joe also went through the game without an intercept. After two weeks he was again atop the NFC in passing.

But then came a very upsetting loss. The Falcons ripped through the 49ers' defense and won, 34–17. Shades of 1980, giving up so many points. Joe was 24 for 34 for 274 yards and two TDs, though this time he also had a pair picked off. One of them was grabbed by safety Tom Pridemore a yard deep in the Falcon end zone, and he promptly returned it 101 yards for a spectacular touchdown. The team was now 1–2. They'd have to get something going soon, because the Falcons were already sitting atop the division at 3–0.

Though the club won the next week, they still didn't look overly impressive. They whipped New Orleans, 21–14, as rookie Ronnie Lott began asserting himself with a 26-yard TD return of an interception. Joe was 16 of 22 for 175 yards and now hitting more than 67 percent of his passes, best in the league.

Next came a 30–17 victory over the Washington Redskins, a game in which the young defensive secondary continued to improve. Dwight Hicks ran eighty yards with a fumble recovery for a touchdown and returned an intercept thirty-two yards for another score. The youthful quartet had intercepted seventeen passes in five games. Joe was 15 of 28 for 193 yards. The club was at 3–2 and seemed to be turning it around.

The following week the San Francisco 49ers came of age. Hosting the always powerful Dallas Cowboys, the Niners were decided underdogs. But they came out smoking. The first time they got the ball Joe took them downfield quickly, culminating the drive with a one-yard toss to Freddie Solomon for the score. Minutes later, Paul Hofer was scoring on a four-yard run. And before the quarter ended, Johnny Davis plunged over from the one. It was already 21–0, and the Cowboys were doing nothing with the Niner defense.

It was a 24–7 game at the half, and in the third period Joe quickly dispelled any thoughts the Cowboys might have for a comeback. He hit Clark on a beautiful 78-yard scoring pass, and before the period ended, Ronnie Lott scored with a 41-yard interception. The final was 45–14, the defense held Dallas star runner Tony Dorsett to twenty-one yards, and Joe was 19 of 29 for 279 yards, a pair of score, and no intercepts. The club was at 4–2, tied for the conference lead, and Joe was its best passer.

"We're maturing, but we're still in the developmental stage," a cautious Bill Walsh told the press. "We still need another strong draft or two, but we're competitive. It's gratifying to see everything going our way for a change."

Joe, too, was very gratified with the way he and the club were playing. But he reminded everyone that they continued to work for it.

"A lot of our success has to do with the offense Coach Walsh has designed for us," he said. "And a lot of it also has to do with the coaches working with the quarterbacks constantly. We never stop working on the fundamentals—drops, protection pockets, where to go when the pocket breaks. We don't leave all that stuff in training camp."

The next week things were a little closer, a 13–3 victory over Green Bay. But it was becoming obvious that the addition of Reynolds, Dean, and the three rookies in the defensive backfield, had made the defensive unit a rather formidable one. Joe had another of his pinpoint accurate games, hitting 23 of 32 for 210 yards and no intercepts. He continued to play simply outstanding football and the club was now in first place in the NFC West at 5–2, with both L.A. and Atlanta at 4–3.

Then came a showdown with the Rams. Joe might have been the Comeback Kid in college, but he much preferred to strike early in the pros, then let the defense do the rest. So in the first period he drove the Niners downfield and hit Solomon for a 14-yard score. Minutes later he tossed a 41-yard TD pass to Clark. That made it 14–0. Then when the Rams came back with ten points of their own, Joe and Earl Cooper hooked up on a 50-yard completion that set up a Wersching field goal and a 17–10 halftime lead.

A field goal by Wersching made it 20–10 in the third. The Rams came back to get it to 20–17, but the Niner defense held them the rest of the way. Joe did it again, 18 of 32 for 287 yards and no intercepts. The club was 6–2, ahead by two games, and unless they did a complete about-face, seemed headed for the playoffs.

By this time, Coach Walsh was totally convinced that he had chosen the right quarterback to run his offense. In fact, he saw his quarterback's future as limitless.

"By 1983 or '84, Joe Montana will be a premier quarterback in the NFL. I'm certain of it," Walsh said, citing the fact that among other things, Joe had set a club record by throwing 99 passes without an intercept.

"Joe is giving the 49ers their best quarterbacking since John Brodie's best days," the coach continued. "I think

Joe's career is going to parallel that of Dan Fouts. Joe may not throw for as many yards because we function differently, but he will be the same as Dan from the standpoint of leadership and efficiency. There was all that talk about his being inconsistent in college, but looking back, I think it may have been the system there, because he certainly hasn't been inconsistent here."

It was also pointed out that many critics had said that all Walsh's quarterbacks did was dump off to their backs. But as Joe matured, he was obviously using his wide receivers a great deal more. His two top receivers after eight games were Dwight Clark and Freddie Solomon.

"Joe always knows where everybody is, or should be, on a given play," the coach said. "He has fantastic downfield vision and instinct. That is the difference between being a mechanical man and a potentially great quarterback. So far, he has done some things we didn't expect to happen until next year or maybe even 1983. But we're not complaining about it."

The 49ers were not about to rest on any laurels. They took another big step in proving they were for real the following week, defeating the powerful Pittsburgh Steelers, 17–14, getting the final score in the last period. Joe had an off game, with two costly intercepts, but the defense, especially those young backs, helped turn it around. Bill Walsh called it "our biggest physical test. Few teams come to Pittsburgh and win."

Win number seven in a row came over Atlanta, 17–14, as Joe threw for two touchdowns and the young secondary again stopped the Falcons with key intercepts. The express was temporarily derailed the next week as the Cleveland Browns upset the 49ers, 15–12. But the club showed its ability to bounce back, winning a key game with the Rams, 33–31, as Joe threw for 283 yards and Ronnie Lott continued his great play with a 25-yard interception return for a TD.

A victory over the Giants, 17–10, brought the Niners

to 10–3 on the year and clinched the NFC West with three weeks still remaining. Joe was 27 for 39 for 234 yards as the club was in the midst of one of the great turnarounds in NFL history. Before the season started the Las Vegas oddmakers said they were 40-to-1 to win their division and 60-to-1 to make the Super Bowl. Well, they reached the first goal. Suddenly, the second didn't seem so out of reach.

From there, the team cruised home. They took a significant victory the next week when they beat the AFC's big turnaround team, the Cincinnati Bengals, 21–3. Joe threw for two TDs and ran for the other. Victories over Houston, 28–6; and the Saints, 21–17, enabled them to finish at 13–3, best record in the history of the franchise, and the best mark in the NFL in 1981.

Bill Walsh was hailed as a genius, and Joe Montana as the game's next great quarterback. Joe finished the regular season with 311 completions in 488 tries for 3,565 yards and an NFL high 63.7 completion percentage. He threw for nineteen touchdowns, had just twelve picked off, and was the NFC passing champion. The overall NFL champ was Ken Anderson of Cincinnati, the first Bill Walsh disciple.

As for Joe's receivers, Dwight Clark led the conference with 85 catches for 1,105 yards and four scores, while Freddie Solomon had 59 grabs for 969 yards and eight scores. So no one could say Joe was a dump-off quarterback anymore. Now the playoffs loomed ahead. In their first game, the Niners would be facing NFC wild card winner, the New York Giants.

By this time, everyone around the NFL knew about Joe Montana, and the great season he had put together. He was called the ideal extension of his coach, in the same way Bart Starr was the ideal extension of Vince Lombardi during the Packer dynasty days. Coach Walsh called Joe one of the greatest ever at hurrying out of the pocket and throwing effectively on the dead run.

And Joe had unending admiration for his coach.

"Coach Walsh continually amazes me," he said. "From what I understand from talking to players on other teams, most of them have the same twenty or twenty-five plays each week. But we've always got new plays as well as dozens of old plays. In many games we'll be prepared to use maybe sixty different plays. One game, I remember, we had more than 100 plays, and that's not counting all our different formations, too."

So Joe had a great deal to learn and execute, and he had accomplished it very quickly. Playing before the home crowd in their first playoff game, the Niners showed they had just too much firepower for the young New York Giants.

Joe got things off in the first period, driving the club downfield and throwing an eight-yard TD pass to Young. But the Giants surprised everyone minutes later when quarterback Scott Brunner hit Earnest Gray on a 72-yard TD bomb, tying the score at 7–7.

The Niners dominated the second quarter. First, Wersching booted a field goal. Then Joe hit Solomon on a 58-yard TD toss, and before the half, Ricky Patton scored on a 25-yard run. So it was 24–10 at the half. The Giants cut it to 24–17 in the third on another long TD pass. But in the final session the Niners put it away. Bill Ring scored one TD from the three, and then the great rookie, Ronnie Lott, ran an intercept twenty yards for another score. The final was 38–24, and the Niners advanced to the NFC title game against the Dallas Cowboys.

Joe had another tremendous game, hitting 20 of 31 for 304 yards and two scores.

"We wanted to get respect or get points, and we got both," said Joe, afterward. "Throwing deep was important because we had to stretch their defense or their great linebackers would keep closing down tighter and tighter until they squeezed the life out of our offense."

But Joe didn't allow them to do that. Now it was the Niners and Cowboys, and in the AFC the Bengals and Chargers. Interestingly enough, of the final four teams, three of them had quarterbacks (Anderson, Fouts, and Montana) developed by Bill Walsh. That should say something about the 49ers' coach's ability.

The Dallas game turned out to be one of the best ever, and a game that would convince any remaining skeptics that Joe Montana had become an absolute first-rate quarterback. Though the Niners had buried Dallas in the regular season they didn't expect to do it again, and they were right.

Joe got the Niners moving on their first possession, driving them sixty-three yards in just six plays, the final one being an eight-yard TD toss to Solomon. The kick made it, 7–0. But the Cowboys were determined not to let this one slip away early. They came right back to get a field goal, and later in the period recovered a Bill Ring fumble and turned it into a 26-yard TD toss from Danny White to Tony Hill. At the end of one the Cowboys led, 10–7.

The clubs traded TDs in the second, the Niners scoring on a 20-yard pass from Joe to Dwight Clark, the Cowboys on a five-yard run by Tony Dorsett. So Dallas had a 17–14 lead at the half. Then in the third period San Francisco converted an interception into their third touchdown, with Johnny Davis plunging over from the two. After three it was 21–17, but it was a long way from over.

A Rafael Septien field goal closed the margin to 21–20 early in the final period. Then midway through the session, the Niners' Walt Easley fumbled at midfield, and the Cowboys drove again, White throwing a 21-yard TD strike to Doug Cosbie. Suddenly, Dallas was ahead, 27–21, with the Doomsday Defense determined to protect the lead. Joe would have to get out his Comeback Kid act if the 49ers were to win.

As time began winding down, Joe started the club moving. But, suddenly, one of his passes was intercepted by Everson Walls, and things looked bleak.

"When they picked that one off, I was scared," Joe said, "real scared."

But the defense held, and Dallas punted to the Niners, who got the ball at their own 11, with 4:54 left. Two plays and Joe was faced with a third and four. He completed a six-yarder to Freddie Solomon. First down. Now the Niners were moving. Joe was mixing his plays well, running his backs, then hitting Clark and Solomon for ten- to twelve-yard gains, as time continued to run down. Finally the ball was at the Dallas 13.

On first down Solomon got open in the end zone, but Joe overthrew him. Could be costly. On second, Lenvil Elliott gained seven yards to the six. Now there were fifty-eight seconds left as the Niners called time out and set up their next play.

The play was for Freddie Solomon, but as Joe looked into the end zone on the left side, he saw Solomon covered. He began sprinting out of the pocket toward the right sideline, looking for Dwight Clark.

"I thought of throwing it away," Joe said, later. "I cocked my arm to do that when I saw Dwight covered. I didn't want to be sacked and take a loss. But just then I saw Dwight getting away from the coverage."

By then Joe was moving backward, had no balance, and had 6-9 Ed "Too Tall" Jones bearing down on him, arms raised. Still, he lofted the pass. Clark, running in front of the end line between two defenders, leaped high and made the catch, as 60,525 fans at Candlestick Park went wild. There were just fifty-one seconds left, but the Comeback Kid had done it. The kick made it 28–27, and the Niner defense held the final seconds, forcing a fumble. San Francisco was in the Super Bowl!

What a game. Charlie Young was calling it the greatest of all time, and the rest of the Niners were just as high. Joe was 22 of 35 for 286 yards and had proved he could really do it in the clutch. As if any old Notre Dame fan didn't know that already.

"Joe does so many intelligent things you can't coach," said Sam Wyche. "He has so much poise and savvy. He just has the right stuff."

It was the biggest throw in 49ers' history, and Clark, who made the catch, explained how he had done it.

"At first I thought it was too high," said the man who had snared eight of Joe's tosses for 120 yards. "I don't jump that well and I was real tired. In fact, I had the flu during the week and had trouble getting my breath on that last drive."

Then how did he catch it?

"How does a lady pick up a car when it's on top of her baby?" he said. "You get it from somewhere."

Now there was one game left for the Niners to complete their rags-to-riches story. They'd be travelling to the Silverdome in Pontiac, Michigan, to face the Cincinnati Bengals and the league's top passer, Ken Anderson, Bill Walsh's first protege. The Bengals, like the Niners, had turned around a 6–10 season in 1980. So they, too, were trying to finish a Cinderella story.

The game took an ominous turn for the 49ers when Amos Lawrence fumbled the opening kickoff and Cincinnati recovered at the San Francisco 26. A quick score would give the Bengals a real shot in the arm. Anderson moved his team to the 11, but then Dwight Hicks picked off a pass at the 5 and returned it all the way to the 32. From there, the Niners drove 68 yards in eleven plays, with Joe running it over himself from the one. Wersching's kick gave S.F. a 7–0 lead. They had turned the game around very quickly.

Early in the second period the Bengals drove again. They moved to the Niner 27 and Anderson threw for his fine rookie receiver, Cris Collinsworth, who made the catch, but was then stripped of the ball by Eric Wright.

The Niners recovered at their own eight. From there, Joe led his club on the longest drive in Super Bowl history, 92 yards in twelve plays, finally hitting Earl Cooper with a scoring pass from the 11 and giving his club a 14–0 lead. Once again they had turned things around. Two Ray Wersching field goals made it 20–0 by halftime.

That was the biggest Super Bowl halftime lead ever, and things looked good. But the Bengals weren't about to quit. They had come too far for that. Anderson marched his team downfield at the beginning of the second half and scored himself on a five-yard run. The kick made it 20–7. Then, near the end of the session they moved again, the big play a 49-yard completion to Collinsworth. Finally, they had first and goal on the San Francisco two-yard line.

Then came another turning point. The Niners made a dramatic goal-line stand, turning back the Bengals four times, and stopping 250-lb. Pete Johnson on the crucial, fourth-down play. That left it at 20–7 after three. But early in the final session, Anderson moved the Bengals downfield and hit tight end Dan Ross for the score. The kick made it 20–14, and suddenly the Bengals were in striking distance.

So the pressure was back on. With 9:57 left, Joe took the ball at his own 27, his best field position of the second half. He moved it carefully and mostly on the ground until Ray Wersching could boot a 40-yard field goal, upping the lead to a safer, 23–14. An Eric Wright interception set up still another field goal. It was now 26–14. The Niners could taste championship. Cincy's last drive came just too late. Anderson threw a TD toss to Ross with sixteen seconds left. That made it 26–21, but the Niners killed the remaining seconds. They had done it. They were World Champs!

Because of the early lead, Joe played a conservative game, completing 14 of 22 for 157 yards. But he had played a flawless game with no interceptions, and was named the Most Valuable Player.

"This is the ultimate goal of football," an overjoyed Joe Montana said in the locker room. "There's a lot of people who played so many years and never got here. And there's a lot who make it and don't win. This has got to be the ultimate. And now we've beaten everybody."

Once again Bill Walsh was full of praise for his quarterback.

"I believe he will be the great football player of the future at quarterback," he said. "He has tremendous quickness of foot, the ability to elude people and still throw accurately. It really paid off today. He made the big difference. He's one of the coolest competitors in the game, one of the greatest instinctive players this game has ever seen and I think he's just getting started."

Coming from others, that might seem just praise of the moment, spoken in victory. But coming from Bill Walsh, the widely acknowledged expert on quarterbacks, it has more than a ring of truth.

Joe had an equal amount of praise for his coach and his teammates, happy that the Niners finally showed everyone what they could really do.

"We won some big games, but the people around the country just didn't seem to believe we had a good team," he said. "Even after we beat Dallas the second time, people still didn't seem to believe in us. Now, I think they do."

It's certain that a lot of people believe in Joe Montana. When he was playing the Comeback Kid at Notre Dame he was just giving people a glimpse of his true potential. It took Bill Walsh and the 49ers to bring the rest of it out in the open.

So things couldn't be better for Joe. He remarried during the 1981 season and has settled down in the Bay Area. He's quarterbacking one of the fine young teams in pro football. If he avoids serious injury, there's a good chance he'll totally fulfill Bill Walsh's prophecy, and become the best around. But with all the fancy words, perhaps it was Freddie Solomon, the mercurial wide receiver, who best summed up the essence of Joe Montana. In low, understated tones, Solomon said simply:

"He always gets the job done."

Amen.

DANNY WHITE

This is the story of Danny White, the outstanding quarterback of the Dallas Cowboys. But it is not his story alone. Whenever you are dealing with a player on the Cowboys, you've also got to deal with the team, a uniquely successful organization, dubbed "America's Team" by some members of the press. In addition, there is also the coach, Tom Landry, the tight-lipped Texan who runs the Cowboys with an iron hand.

And while this is the story of one quarterback, there will also be many references to another. His name is Roger Staubach, a man who became a legend as the Cowboys' signal-caller in the 1970s. Why so many references to Staubach when we're really dealing with Danny White? It's simple. Danny waited for four years to get the Cowboys' job, sitting the bench while Staubach did his thing. The relationship between the two players was often complex and competitive. Yet the two were always friends and very much alike in many ways.

Then there is also the story of the change itself, the passing of the mantle from Staubach to White. In Dallas, it was tantamount to the passing of a royal crown, a coronation, a new monarch taking over from an immensely popular and successful one. So you can imagine the tremendous pressure placed upon Danny White. If he failed, there would be an immediate revolt, a calling for King Roger to retake the throne.

So Danny White knew he would be placed under a microscope, analyzed and dissected, when he took over the team in 1980. The Cowboys had not had a losing season since 1964 and had made it to the Super Bowl five times in the 1970s, winning the big one twice. Should the tradition crumble when Danny White took over, he would have to shoulder the blame, whether it was his fault or not. To put it in a nutshell, Danny White was really on the spot.

There wasn't a football fan anywhere, from the casual to the rabid, who didn't know that Danny was taking over from Staubach in 1980. It was mentioned everywhere. In a sense, it was a football event.

"This is the start of the Danny White Decade," proclaimed Cowboy president Tex Schramm, before the first preseason game of 1980. Talk about great expectations!

Tom Landry, however, did not. The laconic coach put pressure on his new quarterback by taking the opposite approach.

"We've taken a step backward with the retirement of Roger Staubach," he said. "And we may have to take another step backward before we go forward again."

The retiring Staubach also served notice that his successor better be able to cut the mustard.

"What a lot of people don't realize is that you *must* have a good quarterback in the Dallas system," said Roger. "This is imperative. You can't have just another player to fill that position. The machine will not roll along with any quarterback in there."

As for Danny, he was well aware of what he would be up against.

"Taking over for Roger is not like taking over for any other quarterback," Danny said. "The man is a legend and rightfully so, and whoever inherited his position was going to be under a lot of scrutiny, not just locally, but nationally as well. I knew that and I knew I'd have to try to cope with it as best I could."

So that's what Danny White was up against and that's also why his story is not just one of a young quarterback waiting for a chance to play regularly, though that in itself can be a struggle and a frustrating experience, especially to a player who has proved himself in the past and knows he can do the job in the NFL. Sitting on the bench in that situation can be agonizing.

Fortunately, for Danny White, there was a way in which he could participate before he was the regular signal-caller. Being a fine, all-around athlete, Danny had always been an outstanding punter. So while he waited for his chance to do his thing at quarterback, he became the Cowboys' regular punter, and was able to affect the outcome of many games with his foot if not his arm.

But Danny White also felt that when the time came he would be ready. He had the basic training and the track record to go along with it. He even had a father who played in the National Football League.

Wilford Daniel White was born in Mesa, Arizona, on February 9, 1952. His father, Wilford "Whizzer" White, was an all-American halfback at Arizona State, and played for the Chicago Bears in 1951 and '52. Many people think that Danny's dad is a member of the United States Supreme Court, but that is Byron "Whizzer" White, no relation.

At any rate, Danny grew up in Mesa, in a sports oriented atmosphere. Mesa is actually a suburb of Phoenix, so big city sports weren't that far away. It might have been nothing but sports, sports, sports for young Danny had it not been for his mother. Mrs. White insisted that her son take piano lessons, and she started Danny when he was just five years old. Like many youngsters, especially those into sports, Danny didn't like staying inside to practice, but his mother insisted.

He studied the piano for eight years before finally quitting, something he both appreciates and regrets today.

"I took piano lessons for eight years because of my mother and I wish I'd never quit," said Danny, who now plays every day, if possible. "It's a big part of my life again. In fact, I guess it's my secret ambition, to be somebody who could write music, play, and sing."

But when he was young, sports were definitely number one, and Danny played them all. Ironically, he developed faster in baseball, basketball, and track, than in football. In those days, no one really thought that Danny would become a professional football player.

In high school, Danny was a four-sport star, but the three sports in which he was all-State did not include football. In fact, it was a kind of foregone conclusion around Mesa that Danny would be pursuing a career in professional baseball. The proof that he had the goods is simple. At one time or another he was drafted by four major league teams—the Cleveland Indians, New York Mets, Oakland A's, and Houston Astros.

But Danny knew he wanted to go to college. Though he had played quarterback in high school, he was not one of those blue chippers, sought after by dozens of major colleges. He was recruited for baseball and basketball, more than for football. The only two schools that wanted him for football were Brigham Young and Arizona State.

That was an interesting duo. Brigham Young, though not really considered to be among the college gridiron giants, has a reputation for running a pro-type offense and developing NFL caliber quarterbacks. So if Danny had gone to Brigham Young, he would have had a good training ground for the pros.

Only at that time Danny really didn't think much about pro football. Perhaps one reason he chose Arizona State was because of his father, who had gone there

before him. It was his home state school and it also had
a marvelous reputation for turning out baseball players,
the likes of Reggie Jackson, Sal Bando, Rick Monday,
and several others.

On the other hand, if you played football at Arizona
State, you had to deal with Mr. Frank Kush. Coach
Kush was known as perhaps the toughest, meanest, and
most demanding coach in the country. He was ultimate-
ly dismissed and will be coaching at Baltimore in the
NFL for the first time in 1982. Tough as he was, however, Kush had a way of turning out fine football
players, and all have had nothing but praise for the man,
claiming that he made them dig down and bring the talent out from within.

Yet Danny went to Arizona State in the fall of 1970
with a rather unambitious attitude toward football.

"When I got there," he said, "all I wanted to do was
make the team and be the punter. I'd have been happy
just to do that."

But Danny was also a quarterback with a cool head
and a fine arm. Sure enough, it wasn't long before he
won the starting job with the freshman team, and it
wasn't long before he was coming under the critical eye
of Frank Kush.

"The first time I saw Danny White play-the hair stood
up on the back of my neck," the coach confessed. "He
was the kind of young man who didn't make mistake
after mistake after mistake. Plus he wasn't a complainer
and he never criticized anyone or anything. I guess that's
what I liked about him the most."

Then came Danny's sophomore year of 1971. He had
set his sights on being the varsity punter, but if he
thought he could slide through a Frank Kush training
camp just punting the football, he was mistaken. Kush
ran the closest thing to a marine boot camp that college
football had ever seen. It was survival of the fittest, pure
and simple. No way a basically talented quarterback

could slide by and just be a punter.

"Coach Kush made it necessary for you to learn to cope with tough situations," Danny said. "He sometimes really would play havoc with your mind and you had to take it or transfer, or just plain quit. There were times when he'd tell you that you were a lousy, stinking football player who would never make it. Then, later on, you realized he was just using that as a tactic.

"What Coach Kush did my first year with the varsity was make me realize just how good I could be. He forced it out of me, made me want it. I would never have been able to get this talent out of myself without Coach Kush."

It didn't take Danny long to emerge as the starter in 1971. In fact, there was another quarterback there who really expected to be the starter, and when Danny was named, the other player left the team. Danny started the first three games of the 1971 season, and although inexperienced, he began showing qualities of poise and leadership that would follow him into the pros.

But in game three Danny suffered a separated shoulder and went on the shelf for three games. The other quarterback, the one who quit, then rejoined the team and four games later Kush planned to start him against New Mexico, then tied with the Sun Devils for the conference lead. Danny had come off the injured list and was prepared to be the backup.

But five minutes before the game, Coach Kush approached Danny and told him he wanted to take some of the pressure off the other QB, so he wanted Danny to start the game.

"I didn't realize it at the time," Danny said, "but my career was hanging by a thread. Coach Kush told me he wanted me to play just the first series of downs. But if I had had anything but total success, I know he would have yanked me out."

All Danny did that day was move the Sun Devils right

down the field and throw a touchdown pass. Minutes later the team got the ball back and Danny took them down field again before throwing a second scoring aerial. Needless to say, the coach was not about to pull his quarterback then. Before the day was over Danny had thrown six scoring passes and helped Arizona State put sixty points on the scoreboard. The other quarterback quit again, and Danny White was the Sun Devil starter for the rest of his career.

By the time the 1971 season had ended Danny had firmly established himself as a quality quarterback. He completed 86 of 165 passes for 1,393 yards and 15 touchdowns. His completion percentage was 52.1 and he had just nine passes intercepted. He was on his way.

Although he continued to play baseball, football was now the number one sport, the one in which he felt he had the best future. Passing wasn't all he did as a soph. He was also the team's punter, averaging 40.2 yards a kick, and he showed he could run with the ball when he had to. When he returned for his junior year he was even better.

Leading another fine Sun Devil team in 1972, Danny really began to excel. He was 113 of 219 passing, good for 1,930 yards, a 51.6 percentage, and 21 touchdowns. He had fifteen intercepts. He also increased his punting average to 43.0, and generated 2,152 yards total offense. He had even run for a 61-yard touchdown.

By the time he was a senior Danny was a genuine all-America candidate and there was little doubt that he was a winner. At 6-2, and 195 lbs., he had good size and a fine arm. He didn't throw bullets like many young quarterbacks, but exhibited a fine sense of touch, often looping the ball over and between defenders to find his man.

The 1973 season proved to be a record-setting one for Danny White. Before it ended he had set some seven NCAA passing marks. For the year he was 146 of 265, good for 2,609 yards and 23 big touchdowns. His completion percentage was up to 55.1 and he had just twelve passes picked off. He set an NCAA season record with an average gain per passing attempt of 9.85 yards, and his 9.14 career mark was also a record.

In addition, he was second in the nation with 2,862 yards in total offense, and his 8.81 yards per play was also a record, as was his career mark of 8.13. Once again he punted to the tune of a 42.0 average, and he even kicked a couple of extra points, as well as an 80-yard touchdown run. There didn't seem to be anything he couldn't do, and his future as a pro seemed bright. Again, he said he owed it all to Frank Kush.

"If it wasn't for Coach Kush I would probably be riding a bus around Texas playing minor league baseball in the Texas League," he quipped.

Though Danny was to be drafted by the four baseball teams, he never even considered the diamond sport anymore. He waited to see what would happen in the pro football draft. He certainly had the credentials. Including freshman ball, Arizona State had compiled a 32–4 record in the games he started. You can't do much better than that.

When the draft finally came, it didn't take Danny long to get the news. He learned he was a third round pick of the Dallas Cowboys, one of the best teams in the National Football League. There were plenty of college quarterbacks around the country who would have loved to be picked by the Cowboys. Dallas had one of the finest scouting departments in the NFL and their top draft choices were always carefully thought out, players whom the Cowboys felt would work well within their complex system.

It was hard not to know about the Cowboy organization. As recently as the 1970 and 1971 seasons they had made it all the way to the Super Bowl, losing the first time to Baltimore, then whipping Miami to become

World Champs the following year. Danny also knew that the Cowboys had a quarterback named Roger Staubach. A check of the records showed that Staubach had really established himself in 1973, leading the NFL in passing, among other things completing 62.6 percent of his passes and throwing for 23 touchdowns.

So Danny knew that if he joined the Cowboys the chances were he wouldn't be able to dislodge Staubach from the starting post right away, if at all. Because of the competitive fires instilled in him by Frank Kush, that didn't seem like much of a prospect. But then again, there wasn't much choice unless he decided to go to Canada.

However, in 1974, there suddenly was another choice. A new league—the World Football League—was formed to begin play that fall. With the growing popularity of professional football, a group of wealthy businessmen got together to form the new league, hoping there would be enough fans in cities without NFL franchises, and in a few that had existing teams, to support still more ballclubs. After all, that's how the old American Football League started in 1960, and within ten years they had forced a merger with the NFL.

One of the new teams would be located in Memphis, Tennessee. The Memphis Southmen had solid financial backing, and they decided to raid some NFL teams for top talent, rather than just signing castoffs and second stringers. The club pulled a real coup when they grabbed running backs Larry Csonka and Jim Kiick, as well as wide receiver Paul Warfield, from the two-time Super Bowl champion Miami Dolphins.

That made the Southmen legitimate right away. At quarterback, the club signed John Huarte, a former Heisman Trophy winner (1964) from Notre Dame, but a player who had kicked around the NFL for ten years without really establishing himself. Then they made Danny White a top draft choice, and saw in him the chance to develop a young quarterback who could become a real star and a drawing card. The team opened its vaults again and offered Danny twice as much money as the Cowboys.

Danny weighed all the pros and cons of the situation. At Dallas, he'd be with one of the best teams in football, but would he second string at best. If he opted for Memphis, he'd be making more money and would have a chance to start. But he'd be playing in an inferior league, one which might not survive economically, if it did artistically. Finally, he decided that the amount of money was worth the risk. He signed a multi-year contract with Memphis of the WFL.

One thing Danny was right about. At Memphis he played. He shared playing time with Huarte, but slowly emerged as the stronger player and was starting by the end of the 1974 season. He was also the league's top punter. Had the league survived, Danny might very well have stayed there, but midway through the 1975 season the World Football League collapsed, for a variety of reasons.

Danny had certainly established himself statistically. In a season and a half he had completed 183 of 350 passes for 2,635 yards and 21 touchdowns. Having met with professional success, even if it was the WFL, Danny didn't feel so good about being out of a job midway through his second pro season. He learned quickly, however, that the rights to the college players who had opted for the WFL, still belonged to the NFL teams that had drafted them. So he had another opportunity to negotiate with the Cowboys and soon signed a contract to play in Dallas in 1976.

Now it was time to study the Cowboy situation more closely. The club was an expansion team joining the NFL in 1960, the same year the AFL was formed. At that time, there were just twelve NFL teams. The Cowboys made the thirteenth, and were followed by the

Minnesota Vikings a year later. In their first season of play, Dallas didn't win a game, finishing at 0–11–1, the worst expansion record ever until the Tampa Bay Buccaneers finished at 0–14 in 1976.

At any rate, it was the first of five losing seasons for the Cowboys. But the club had a tough-minded coach who believed in his system and had the patience to slowly accumulate the players to carry it out. His name was Tom Landry, a former defensive back with the New York Giants, who had served as an assistant coach there until he moved to Dallas as head man. He's been with the Cowboys ever since, the one and only coach in franchise history.

By 1965 Landry had the Cowboys at the break-even point, finishing with a 7–7 mark. A year later they won the NFL Eastern Division title at 10–3–1 and four years later they were headed to the first of their five trips to the Super Bowl. Once Landry got his club to the top, he kept them there. Unlike most teams, which have periods of decline and transition as new players replace old, the Cowboys have maintained their level of excellence without letup. It seems whenever a top-flight player retired, Landry and the Cowboy brass would have another to take his place.

The first Cowboys' quarterback was Eddie LeBaron, a scrappy little guy who had already achieved moderate success in the NFL before coming to the expansion Cowboys. Also joining the team at the beginning was an all-American rookie signal-caller out of Southern Methodist University, Don Meredith.

Dandy Don at first alternated with LeBaron, then took over the helm. During those first tough years, Meredith took a real beating, but hung in there to ride the Cowboys when they started winning, taking the team to the NFL title game on several occasions.

Despite a first-rate quarterback like Meredith, Coach Landry was always looking ahead. In 1964 he drafted a strong-armed QB from the University of California, Craig Morton, and the next year he surprised everyone by taking Roger Staubach of the Naval Academy.

Why a surprise? Simple. Staubach had a four-year obligation to the Navy, and wouldn't be able to join the Cowboys until 1969. Several previous service academy players had tried to return to pro ball after a four-year absence, and none had really made it. But the Cowboys saw something special in Staubach and they decided to take the risk.

Roger left the Navy after serving in Vietnam, and reported to the Cowboys in 1969. That was to be Don Meredith's last year, with Morton still on hand as the heir apparent. There's a story that Dandy Don, after watching Staubach pushing himself hour after hour, striving to make up for lost time and still improve, turned to Morton and said:

"Old Roger's gonna get your job, Craig."

That might be part of the Cowboys' folklore, but it very well could have happened. For Staubach was a dedicated performer with a wealth of natural talent. Yet he didn't get the job overnight. Because of the complexity of the Dallas system, Coach Landry rarely played rookies. In fact, a player often needed several years to learn the offense or defense, especially at the so-called skilled positions.

It wasn't until Staubach's fifth season that he finally had the job free and clear. He had been on the brink of getting it in 1971, finishing the season as the regular, then was hurt the following year. So it wasn't until 1973 that he really established himself as one of the NFL's best. He was 31 years old then, not young, but certainly in his prime. That was the same year Danny came out of Arizona State and opted for the WFL.

So when Danny finally joined the Cowboys in 1976, the 34-year-old Staubach still remained. Only Roger was a very young 34, an extremely dedicated athlete who lived clean and kept himself in marvelous physical condition. Danny knew he wouldn't be playing right away. In fact, there really was no timetable. Sure, he'd try his hardest to beat Staubach out, but Danny also knew the reality of the situation. He also knew he never liked being a backup quarterback.

"No, I was never happy being a backup," he said. "When I signed with the Cowboys there was a real excitement in just being there, being part of the team. But once that wore off I wanted to play. After all, I had nearly two successful years in the World Football League and that gave me confidence.

"But I think the toughest thing eventually was living with that name—backup quarterback. I found myself being introduced that way all the time until I really wanted to scream. It got so every time I heard the term it brought all my frustrations to the surface."

There was another young quarterback with the Cowboys that year, Clint Longley, who had been backing up Staubach for a couple of years and figured he was the next to get the job. Danny saw what the frustration of waiting could do to someone.

"I remember that Longley had a great arm," Danny said, "but something in him seemed to turn sour the year I came. I guess that had something to do with it. With me there he couldn't be sure that he was the heir apparent anymore. It changed him. He wouldn't even work out with us."

Longley eventually had a much-publicized fist fight with Staubach and wasn't with the Cowboys much longer after that. But Danny soon became fast friends with Jolly Roger. The two were a lot alike. They had similar lifestyles, both clean living, dedicated athletes, devoted to their families, and with a strong belief in God. It was these similarities that undoubtedly allowed them to remain close while both knew that Danny wanted that number one job.

There was one thing that kept Danny from really going stir crazy. He quickly won the punting job and right from the start proved to be one of the more reliable kickers in the league. Landry also loved the idea that his punter could throw the football if need be. Danny found another way to work off the frustration of not playing regularly. He began really pushing himself on the weight machines.

"I'd kill myself on those machines," he said. "By the end of that first year I could press 275 pounds. Of course, I had my family to come home to. That was really the best thing. My wife, Jo Lynn, and my two sons were great. Take the kids. They couldn't have cared less whether I played or not, or whether I had a good or bad game. All they knew was their Daddy was home."

The Cowboys had their usual solid team in 1976. There were few weaknesses. Offensively, the line featured the likes of John Fitzgerald, Pat Donovan, Herbert Scott, and Tom Rafferty. Receivers Drew Pearson and Billy Joe Dupree were first rate, and running backs Robert Newhouse and Preston Pearson did a fine job.

Defensively, the team was potentially awesome, with the likes of Ed "Too Tall" Jones, Randy White, and Harvey Martin anchoring the line. Veterans Bob Breunig, D.D. Lewis, and Thomas "Hollywood" Henderson were the linebackers, while Cliff Harris, Charlie Waters, and Benny Barnes anchored the secondary. There was no way this club wouldn't be in the thick of the fight, especially with Tom Landry and his fine staff running the show.

The club opened the season against the Philadelphia Eagles, then beginning to rebuild under Coach Dick Vermeil. The Eagles were no match for the Dallas powerhouse, and the Cowboys had a substantial lead by halftime. With the score still one-sided late in the game, Coach Landry decided to put his new quarterback in.

So Danny got a taste of action in his first NFL game. Right away he showed the coolness and poise that had always characterized his play. Though the game was won and a club usually keeps the ball on the ground in these situations, Landry wanted Danny to get the feel of throwing in the NFL, so he called a number of short passes. By game's end, Danny had completed five of the seven he threw, for just twenty-five yards. But this was a good way to begin.

The problem was that getting into the season opener really whetted his appetite, and when Danny saw no more quarterback action for more than a month it was difficult to take. On October 24, the 5–1 Cowboys were playing the Chicago Bears. Midway through the game Staubach hurt his passing hand. Suddenly, Danny got the call while the game was still on the line.

Did he ever respond! With Landry calling the plays from the sideline as usual, Danny executed them to perfection. He completed seven of 10 passes for 145 big yards and two touchdowns to lead the club to a 31–21 victory. Though he also threw a pair of intercepts, no one could easily fault his performance. The victory gave the Cowboys a 6–1 mark and sole possession of first place in the NFC East.

A week later Staubach was forced to go against the Washington Redskins, who were just a game behind the Cowboys. Dallas won it, 20–7, though Staubach's hand was still hurting. So when the lowly New York Giants were the next team on the schedule, Danny assumed he'd get the start, allowing Staubach's hand to heal. But it wasn't until the team had lined up for the pre-game introductions that Danny knew for sure that Roger, bad hand and all, was still the starter. That got to him.

"It was a real blow to me," he admitted, later. "I began to feel that the coach didn't have any confidence in me at all. If the Cowboys believed that Roger was better injured than I was healthy, then I began to think that maybe I belonged somewhere else."

So it didn't take long for the frustration of being the

backup to surface. It's funny how a player can accept his role under certain circumstances, but the acceptance is always held by a very fragile thread. This time it snapped because of the anticipation of a start that never came. Danny got into just one other game in the end of November 1976, throwing one pass for 43 yards against St. Louis.

Otherwise, he just punted and sat, while the Cowboys won another NFL East title with an 11–3 record. For the season, Danny had completed 13 of 20 passes for 213 yards and a pair of scores. It wasn't much for a guy who had been a regular for five straight years, three at Arizona State and two in the WFL. But he basically knew this would happen when he joined the Cowboys, at least for a year or so.

He did punt well, kicking seventy times for a 39.4 average, so he didn't allow his frustrations to affect that part of his game. Unfortunately, the Cowboys lost in the first round of the playoffs that year, falling to the L.A. Rams, 14–12. Now it was on to 1977. With Roger Staubach at 35-years-old, how much longer could he go on?

The Cowboys had one important addition to their offense in '77. They made a trade which brought them the league's top draft choice, and they used it to grab Tony Dorset, the record-setting halfback from Pittsburgh who had won the Heisman trophy in his senior year. Dorsett was the break-away runner the team lacked. They also added wide receiver Tony Hill from Stanford. He wouldn't play much as a rookie, but would become a gamebreaker in his own right the following year.

In addition, the club acquired kicker Rafael Septien and another quarterback, Glenn Carano of Nevada-Las Vegas, at 6-3, 202-lbs. with a very strong arm. Now Danny had someone both in front and behind him. Still, he kept his cool, hoping to see more action in 1977.

What he found himself doing was punting for perhaps

the best team in all of football. Staubach, at age 35, was still a marvelous, durable quarterback, a strong thrower who still knew how to run when he had to, and had the guts to take the big gamble with the game on the line. In fact, there are many who felt that Roger Staubach was the most dangerous quarterback ever in the final two minutes at a ballgame and with his team behind, yet in striking distance.

Pulling out games in the final seconds became a Staubach and a Cowboy trademark. So no matter how you looked at it, Danny White was sitting behind one of the best. He got into parts of just three games all year, as the Cowboys rode to a fine, 12–2, record and won the division by three full games. Danny was just four of 10 for 35 yards all season long. His punting average improved to 39.6, but that had to be small consolation. What he really wanted to do was play quarterback.

Interestingly enough, though there had to be frustration for Danny, he and Roger Staubach were becoming even closer. A further irony was Staubach's own statement when he joined the Cowboys as a rookie, back in '69. At that time he saw how close Don Meredith and Craig Morton were.

"I don't think I could be that friendly with a guy whose job I was trying to take," Roger had said.

Of course, now he had the job and the fact that Danny didn't resent him personally, showed the kind of mold Danny White was cut from.

"Danny was always very understanding of his role," Staubach said. "We really had a deep respect for each other as athletes right from the beginning. I told him I wasn't going to hang on until they had to drag me off the field. I also knew what Danny was going through since I had gone through the same thing myself. And I also knew how important Danny was to the Dallas Cowboys.

"I guess the bottom line is that we can both get the job

done in different ways," Staubach continued. "I always enjoyed being Danny's friend. He has a great deal of depth and while he might not be the overbearing competitor I am, he certainly competes. It's just more subtle with him, but it's in him and it's strong."

Off the field, the two would compete in everything, even in ping pong. To many observers, it was like a big-brother-little-brother thing, which Danny confirmed on many occasions.

"Sure, there were times when I resented being the backup. But the flareups were always brief. And I was well aware that Roger hadn't talked his way into the job. He earned it. He was a great quarterback, the best, and I learned a lot just being around him. I watched the way he handled the media and all the attention he always got, and my admiration for him just kept growing.

"Then, of course, there would be Monday mornings after a game. That was the worse part, waking up and not aching anywhere. You felt as if you hadn't done anything. So even though we were friends, I was never satisfied just being the punter."

But the punter he was in 1977. And as the punter he certainly would play an important role in the upcoming playoffs, with field position often crucial in close games. There was little hope of quarterbacking unless Staubach was hurt, and Danny didn't want that. Roger had again led the NFC in passing, completing 58.2 percent of his tosses and throwing just nine intercepts in sixteen games. Rookie runner Dorsett, incidentally, had lived up to his notices. He didn't start until midway through the season and still managed to gain more than 1,000 yards.

The team showed its power in the first playoff game, easily defeating Chicago, 37–7. Then, in the NFC title game, they beat Minnesota handily, 23–6. It was hard to envision anyone stopping the well-oiled Cowboy machine. In Super Bowl XII the Cowboys would be facing the Denver Broncos, who were quarterbacked by ex-Cowboy Craig Morton.

Dallas drew first blood in the opening period. A pass interception by Randy Hughes gave the Cowboys the ball at the Denver 25. Five plays later Dorsett ran it in from the three. The point made it 7–0. Before the quarter ended, a Dallas field goal made it 10–0, and another field goal in the second quarter gave the Cowboys a 13–0 lead at the half.

Denver made a run in the third period, getting a field goal and a touchdown, but in between Staubach hit Butch Johnson on a 45-yard scoring pass, as Johnson made a diving catch in the end zone. That made it 20–10, and a final score on a Robert Newhouse option pass to Golden Richards made the final, 27–10. The Cowboys were World Champs.

Danny entered late in the game, hitting one of the two passes he threw, and running once for thirteen yards. It wasn't much, but he had played in a Super Bowl, had been on the winning team and received the prestigious ring that so many players covet and never get. It had to be a somewhat satisfying experience. Now he would just hope his time was coming.

Basically, however, 1978 was more of the same. The Cowboys were on the way to a third straight NFC East title, this time with a 12–4 mark. Going into the regular season finale with the New York Jets Danny had again thrown the ball just ten times all year. Staubach, however, was pretty much banged up and Coach Landry decided to rest him for the playoffs. That gave Danny the first start of his NFL career.

He made the most of it, completing 15 of 24 passes and executing with his usual precision as the Cowboys won, 30–7. That left his season log at 20 of 34 for 215 yards, no touchdowns, and one intercept. Not much to write home about. Deep inside, Danny's frustration was growing.

There was a wild card playoff game in 1978, so that the Cowboys had an extra week of rest before their first playoff contest. By the time they were ready to meet the Atlanta Falcons Staubach was rested and ready. Danny was back on the bench. The Falcons were a tough bunch, with a bomb-throwing quarterback named Steve Bartkowski and a young, aggressive defense. They could hurt you.

The Falcons were really up for the game and they took a 20–13 lead as the first half wore down. Dallas had the ball and Staubach dropped back to pass. Atlanta blitzed and there was a huge pileup. When they unstacked, one player wasn't getting up—Roger Staubach. The QB had been knocked unconscious and had to be helped from the field. Suddenly, Danny was in the game and on the spot. The half quickly ended and he learned in the locker room that Staubach had a concussion and would be unable to return. It would be up to Danny to pull the game out.

It was the most pressure-filled situation he had been in since joining the team. Determined to help the young quarterback, the Dallas Doomsday Defense tightened up. They would hold the Falcons if Danny would get the points. Midway through the third period the Cowboys took over on the Falcon 46. Danny came in and got the club moving.

He engineered a beautiful drive, executing both pass and running plays well and moving the club smoothly. Six plays later he had the ball down to the two-yard line. He took the snap from center and dropped back, looking at the players as they criss-crossed. Finally he spotted reserve tight end Jackie Smith and fired. Touchdown! Danny had brought the club in. Rafael Septien's kick tied the game at 20.

In the final session the Cowboy defense continued to hold tight. Then with some twelve minutes left, Atlanta's John James shanked a punt. The ball went just ten yards, giving it to Dallas on the Falcon 30. Danny came on again and five plays later gave the ball to fullback Scott Laidlaw, who plunged in for the go-ahead score. Septien's kick made it 27–20. There was still some 9:46 left, but Danny and the offense played ball control and the defense continued to hold Atlanta. When it ended, Dallas had a 27–20 victory and Danny White had proved he could produce under pressure.

Under the circumstances Danny had done extremely well. He completed 10 of 20 passes for 127 yards and a touchdown. The Falcons intercepted one of his passes, but did no damage with it. It had to be the happiest moment of his Cowboy career.

The next week, however, Staubach was recovered and went most of the way in the NFC title game, a 28–0 thrashing of the Rams. Roger also went the distance in Super Bowl XIII, an exciting affair that saw the Cowboys lose to Pittsburgh, 35–31, though Staubach's late heroics again made it close. Still, there was no doubt about the overall quality of the team. It was still excellent, close to the best.

Now came 1979 and Danny White was getting restless. There had been some Staubach retirement rumors during the offseason, but Roger quickly scotched them. At age 37, he'd be back for still another campaign. Danny was going into his fourth year with the club. He didn't know how much longer he could wait. He had never issued any play-me-or-trade-me ultimatums, but it had to be somewhere in the back of his mind if things didn't change. After all, what if Staubach continued to play until he was forty. Some quarterbacks had done it, and Roger was certainly in as good a condition and still worked as hard as anyone. He just didn't know.

When it became obvious that 1979 was going to be more of the same, Staubach pitching and White waiting in the bullpen, the situation started eating at Danny worse than ever. Being called a backup quarterback stuck in his craw as never before. And other little, seemingly insignificant things began to really bug him.

"We would be sitting in the meeting room, looking at a film, and it was as if I wasn't there," Danny recalled. "The coaches would say things like, 'Roger, look at this,' and 'Roger, look at that.' I used to sit there hoping they would say just once, 'Quarterbacks, look at this.'

"Another time the coaches handed out a performance sheet which graded everyone in certain areas, showing us things that had to improve. I remember one of them saying that the first priority was to 'protect Roger,' not 'protect the quarterbacks.' I pasted that one up on my locker and I'd look at it before practice and get all fired up."

As the season wore on, the Cowboys were fighting the Eagles and Redskins for the division lead and maybe even for a playoff berth. The team wasn't playing as consistently as it had in the past, and at one point in the middle of the year they dropped three straight games. That's when Danny decided to pay Coach Landry a visit.

"I didn't demand to be traded or anything like that," Danny said. "I really didn't want that. I didn't want to move my family around. That kind of thing is always a risk. Of the twenty-seven other places I could go, maybe I'd be happy in four of them. On the other hand, there comes a time when you have to decide if you're going to be a starter or a backup for the rest of your career.

"What I didn't want was Coach Landry and the rest of the staff to think that I was content to be a backup quarterback. I wanted to play very badly and I wanted him to know it. With the team losing three in a row I just felt it was a good time to talk about it. He just listened to what I had to say and then he told me he wished he had more players who wanted to start as badly as I did. But there was no kind of commitment."

Though Danny was very frustrated and still down about the situation, his friendship with Staubach continued. In fact, he once remarked that the problem all those years was that "I could never get mad enough at Roger to beat him out." He quickly added, diplomatically, "Not that I could have."

The Cowboys, of course, were known as America's Team. Danny would joke with Roger, calling him America's Quarterback, and soon Staubach was giving it right back, referring to Danny as America's Punter. But eventually it was Staubach himself who gave Danny a hint that things might soon change.

"Roger started talking to me one day during the season and he kind of hinted that he would not be back in 1980," Danny said. "He told me to just hang in there and wait for my turn."

Still, there was the 1979 season to worry about. Despite his frustrations, Danny continued to punt, and punt well. In fact, he was having his finest year as a punter, vying for the NFC lead during most of the season. And what the season finally came down to was one, final game. The Cowboys had beaten the Eagles in the fifteenth game, and now three teams, the Eagles, Cowboys, and Redskins, were all even at 10–5. Two would make the playoffs and one would likely be out, though the wild card possibilities were very complex. But they couldn't all tie because the Cowboys and Redskins would be meeting head to head.

The way it turned out the Cowboys had to win to get in the playoffs. And for most of the game it looked as if they wouldn't. The Skins took the early lead, only to have Dallas storm back with three scores to go in front, 21–17. Then Washington rallied behind quarterback Joe Theismann for a field goal and two touchdowns. They had a 34–21 advantage with less than four minutes remaining.

And that's when Roger Staubach did his thing. At age 37, he showed again that he was still the most dangerous last-minute quarterback in the game. With the whole season, a trip to the playoffs, all of it on the line,

Staubach calmly engineered two touchdown drives in the final four minutes to pull the game out, 35–34. It gave the Cowboys an 11–5 mark and yet another divisional crown.

Danny finished the year the second best punter in the NFC with a 41.7 average. He had become extremely proficient at kicking the ball out of bounds inside the 20, and his kicks were rarely run back for big yardage. As a quarterback, however, it was a familiar story. He threw just 39 passes all season, completing 19 for 267 yards, one touchdown, and two interceptions. In four NFL seasons he had thrown just 103 passes. Some NFL quarterbacks now throw that many in two weeks. It's not difficult to imagine how he must have felt.

He also had to wonder, watching Roger Staubach's heroics in that final game, whether he'd ever have the number one job. Staubach was like Old Man River, he just rolled along, aging like fine wine. The man actually seemed better than ever. When the season ended he was the leading passer in the entire National Football League.

The Cowboys had to meet the Los Angeles Rams in the first NFC playoff game. Though they had been in the last two Super Bowls, they weren't about to make it three straight. The Rams beat them, 21–19, to knock the Cowboys out of the playoffs. So Danny packed it in for another year, wondering just what the future would bring.

But the big decision during the off season was Staubach's. The consensus of opinion seemed to be that Roger should return. It seemed as if everyone wanted him back, the fans, his teammates, the coaches. There was little doubt that he could go again . . . except possibly for one thing. Roger had sustained a number of concussions over the past several seasons and that always prompted some caution.

Whether that was a factor or not is hard to say, but

in March of 1980 the announcement came. Roger Staubach was retiring!

How long Danny had waited to hear that. In fact, when the smoke had cleared, Staubach indicated that one reason he was going was because of Danny.

"I could have played one more year," he said, "but there was no way I could feel guilty about leaving the Cowboys when Danny was so ready to play. I don't think the Cowboys will miss a beat with Danny White."

Roger did leave the door slightly ajar, saying that he would stay in condition just in case of an emergency. What that meant is hard to say. Perhaps if Danny had suffered a serious injury in training camp, say something that required surgery, perhaps then Staubach would have come back. But when he retired, he meant it.

Of course, Staubach's announcement was just the beginning of the hoopla. This was not your average case of an athlete retiring and another moving in to take his place. This was Dallas, Texas, where things are done in a big way. As Cowboy president Tex Schramm said, "Roger was more than a great quarterback. He was a national hero. He epitomized everything that's good about this country. Everybody loved him, not just the football fans. To most people, Roger was the Dallas Cowboys."

Talk about replacing a legend. Staubach's announcement had changed Danny's life overnight. No longer was he Danny White, backup quarterback, who could live his life out of the spotlight. Now he was the man replacing Staubach, and the media people came swarming after him. Fortunately, he would still be able to go to his friend for advice and reassurance.

"I talked to Roger about what would happen," Danny said, "and he told me he couldn't really explain what it would be like. It was something I couldn't anticipate but would have to learn to go through. He said it would be hard and he was right."

Even before training camp started there were analyses and comparisons between the abdicating king and the heir apparent. Tex Schramm put it this way.

"One of the reasons for our great success in the 1970s was the tremendous confidence everybody in the organization had in Roger Staubach. Everyone felt that no matter what happened, in the end Roger would somehow find a way to win the game. When a player who has been such an integral part of a team departs, the personality of that team can never be quite the same. That's not to say we can't be as successful. We just won't be the same. But the Cowboys of the 1980s will now adapt to Danny White."

Wide receiver Drew Pearson, the man Staubach always seemed to find open in those life-or-death situations, also knew the club would have to readjust.

"To say that we have as much confidence in Danny as we did in Roger at this point would be ridiculous," Pearson said. "But don't forget, we've worked with Danny for four years and we all know what he can do."

As for the quiet man, Tom Landry, he, too, felt Danny was ready. In fact, he felt he was more than ready.

"I think a quarterback reaches a point where he simply has to play," Landry said. "Danny White has reached that point. If Roger had said he wanted to play another year or two, I'm sure we would have lost Danny. This probably would have been the year. There is an obligation to a player like Danny White, or Craig Morton before him, to give him the chance to play or allow him to move on to a place where he will fit in."

Even the lifestyles of the two quarterbacks off the field were being compared. Part of one article said:

"They are both short-haired, non-swearing straight arrows who dote on their families. Neither man smokes nor drinks. They are both deeply involved in the church but reluctant to talk about it for fear of coming off as goody-goodies."

The same article pointed out that while both quarter-backs were soft-spoken, they took charge on the field. They were leaders, and neither had ever experienced a losing season in football.

"With Roger it seemed that guys were always making impossible catches, going beyond themselves," said Tex Schramm. "I don't know if there is a physical explanation for it. It's just that some guys are born winners and it rubs off on the people around them. Roger had that quality and Danny has it, too.

"Danny always gives the impression that he's totally in command. He's poised and has that little twinkle in his eye that says he just might throw the bomb on third and inches. He's quiet on the outside, but you can tell he's tough as nails on the inside."

Tom Landry put the comparison in more technical terms. "Roger had a great arm and the great confidence to throw into a tight spot," the coach said. "Danny tends to watch a lot more of what is going on and uses everything at his disposal. Danny isn't as strong a thrower as Roger. But if he uses all his people he will be able to make up for that. He also has the same type of character as Roger. He's confident and a leader, and thus has the same mental qualities that Roger possesses."

Finally it was time to put all the talk to rest and play the game. Training camp opened and the Cowboys once again had a talented football team. Danny certainly had the tools to work with. His offensive line was a veteran unit, totally familiar with the Cowboy offense. Halfback Dorsett had run for more than 1,000 yards in each of his three seasons, while Robert Newhouse was a reliable and often underrated fullback. In addition, a fine rookie named Ron Springs could play either backfield position.

Veteran Drew Pearson and the explosive Tony Hill were the wide receivers, with the often spectacular Butch Johnson in reserve. Billy Joe Dupree was a clutch-catching tight end, with Jay Saldi and rookie Doug Cosbie ready to spell him or join him in short yardage situations. The Doomsday Defense was still solid, with a possible weak spot in the defensive backfield with the sudden retirement of safety Cliff Harris.

Danny was running with the first unit right away, and it felt good. Now Glenn Carano was the backup, and believe it or not, there were already stories about Carano's strong arm and how he might soon challenge for the job. But knowing Tom Landry, there was no way Danny wouldn't get a full and total shot at running the team.

There were some 55,000 fans at Texas Stadium to watch the first preseason game of 1980 against the Green Bay Packers. Many of them were there for one basic reason; to see how Danny White would fare in his initial start as the Cowboys' number one quarterback.

If Danny was nervous, he didn't show it. He came out on the field like a seasoned veteran, calm and poised, and ready to go to work. But anyone following the Cowboys knew this had been Danny's demeanor for four years, no matter how brief his appearances. There really should be no reason to change now. And when he began running the Dallas offense, a lot of fans let out a collective sigh of relief.

Danny was playing very well. At one point, Tony Hill ran a sideline pattern, then cut sharply over the middle. To hit him, Danny would have to get the ball between two, fast-closing defenders. It was the kind of pass Staubach had completed so often, almost routinely. Danny saw the play developing, cranked and threw. The ball hummed over the middle where Hill grabbed it on the run for a 19-yard gain and a first down. He had passed another test. The throw had more than enough zip on it.

By the time Danny gave way to Carano, he had played a little more than a half, completing seven of 13 passes for 99 yards. He was on the field for both Dallas touchdowns in a 17–14 victory. On two occasions he scrambled out of the pocket to avoid being sacked, and turned the play into big gains. One time he ran for eleven yards, and the other time he tossed a 24-yard strike to Jay Saldi.

The Cowboys won their first three preseason games, with Danny playing very well in all of them. The final tuneup would be with those powerful Pittsburgh Steelers, who were defending Super Bowl champs for the fourth time in six years. The game was at Texas Stadium and some 62,000 fans were on hand to see how their team and their new quarterback could cope with the Steel Curtain.

Unfortunately, the Cowboys and Danny didn't cope too well. It was a Pittsburgh night nearly all the way. One of Danny's problems was that the Cowboy offensive line broke down, and he often found himself running for his life. He threw two intercepts, and a possible third, which was run back eighty yards by Steeler lineman Gary Dunn, was called back by the referee.

What it amounted to was a 31–3 Pittsburgh victory which undoubtedly left many witnesses muttering something about Roger Staubach returning. Actually, Danny didn't do badly in the first half, hitting eight of 19 for 105 yards. But everything went haywire after intermission. Maybe the Cowboys and Danny were entitled to a bad game. Now they'd have to forget and get ready to open the regular season against the always tough Washington Redskins at RFK Stadium.

It would be very hard for Danny to keep a low profile. Every NFL preview story focused on the quarterback changeover at Dallas. One headline read, "Can America's Team Survive the Switch?" The story made a point of how the Cowboys had always replaced all-pro players without any loss of team efficiency. It then hinted that this could be the exception.

To make matters worse, the opener was a Monday night game and would be seen on national television. Fortunately, for Danny, the Cowboy defense made it easy, stifling the Redskin attack all night. With that to work with, Danny was able to execute a fairly conservative game plan, good for his first outing, and lead the club to a 17–3 victory. He was 10 of 18 for 107 yards. He didn't throw a touchdown, however, and had a pair of passes picked off. But overall, things went well.

Not so for the team the following week. After playing at Washington Monday night, they had to travel to Denver for a game with the Broncos the following Sunday. Coach Landry didn't like it at all.

"I've said many times that a team that travels for a Monday night game should be home the following week. The Monday night games takes too much out of the players if they have to go right back on the road again."

Landry was right. At Denver, the Cowboys collapsed. The Broncos converted three turnovers into touchdowns and walked away with the game, 41–20. Very few of the Cowboys played well. But one exception was Danny White.

Danny was magnificent all afternoon, trying to rally his team, and never quitting, even when it seemed the game was out of hand. He completed 20 of 34 passes for 292 yards and two scores. Both were to Tony Hill, one covering 36 yards, the other 22. Even in defeat Danny had achieved more in one game than he had in any of his four previous seasons.

The following week the team came home to face the Tampa Bay Buccaneers. Midway through the second period the Bucs had taken a 17–7 lead. But Danny White wasn't about to let this one get away. He calmly directed three long scoring drives, one in each period, as the defense shut the door at the same time and Dallas won, 28–17.

It had to be a sweet win for both the club and their fans. Danny seemed to really take control. He completed 24 of 33 passes for 244 yards, didn't have any picked off, and threw for three scores, including a 28-yarder to Butch Johnson. Tony Dorsett ran for 100 yards to balance the attack. As tight end Jay Saldi said:

"You can't compare Danny to Roger Staubach yet, but he's the best quarterback we have and a born leader. Win or lose, we believe in him."

Speaking of Staubach, the ironic thing was that when the two were competing on the field, Danny never got angry with Roger. Yet during the preseason, when Roger was doing color commentary on the Cowboy games for a regional network, he second-guessed Danny on a couple of plays, and that irked the younger man.

"It's funny," Danny said, "I don't mind criticism when it comes from John Brodie (another ex-quarterback-turned-broadcaster), but it bothered me coming from Roger. I guess it's the old competitive thing between us coming out again. But to me it was as if Roger was saying, 'Well, I could have done it better.' "

The next week was a nice, neat win over the Packers, 28–7. Dallas scored a touchdown in each period as Danny threw with pinpoint accuracy, completing 16 of 20 for 217 yards and two scores. After four weeks he had completed 70 of 105 passes for an amazing, 66.7 completion percentage. He had seven TDs and just three intercepts, and was the top-rated passer in the NFC, second in the overall NFL. You couldn't ask for much better than that.

Next came two easy wins, over the Giants and 49ers. In fact, the 49ers' game was a 59–14 romp in which Danny was 16 of 22 for 239 yards and four scores. But the club was headed for a showdown game with the Eagles. They had to forget the easy ones. Both clubs were at 5–1 and vying for the lead in the NFC East.

It was one of those bone-crunching games from start to finish. Dallas took a 7–0 lead in the first quarter when linebacker Mike Hegman recovered an Eagle fumble in the end zone. A Tony Franklin field goal cut it to 7–3, and Philly took a 10–7 lead before Rafael Septien booted a three-pointer to tie it by the half.

After a scoreless third period, Philly managed to punch it across midway through the final session to take a 17–10 lead. As time was running down, Danny had the Cowboys moving. With less than two minutes left, Dallas had a first and goal just inside the Philly 10. Then a first down pass to Drew Pearson in the end zone was broken up by cornerback Roynell Young.

Second down, Danny passed over the middle, and linebacker Bill Bergey was there to bat it away. Third down saw a swing pass to rookie running back James Jones, but it gained just two. Now it was fourth and goal from the eight. Again Danny went to the air. He tried to lob one to Tony Hill in the back corner of the end zone, and again Roynell Young made the play. The Eagles had held and were able to run out the clock for the victory.

Danny was 20 of 38 for 222 yards, but he was intercepted three times and didn't get the score from inside the 10 in those final minutes. There had to be people who said Roger would have gotten the team in. Danny probably thought of it as well, but he was also confident in his own abilities and would just grit his teeth and go back to work.

He and his teammates came back to win a big one, whipping the high-powered Chargers, 42–21. Danny was 22 of 34 for 260 yards and three scores. So Danny's first season as a starter was half over and he had his club at 6–2. He had completed 150 of 232 passes for 1,847 yards, a 64.7 percentage, 16 touchdowns and eight intercepts. He was the second leading passer in the NFL, behind Vince Ferragamo of Los Angeles. He was really earning the respect of his teammates.

"I remember the first game against Washington," said Billy Joe Dupree. "Danny called ten or twelve audibles. Roger didn't even do that often. Roger was such a great competitor that he figured he'd make the play work even if the defense was stacked against it. Danny hasn't got to that stage yet. But he's gutsy. He isn't afraid to change the play."

Coach Landry commented that "Danny uses everything at his disposal. He's confident and a leader."

And Danny himself said, "The way I look at it, if you're going to beat me you've got to beat everything I've got, everything I can do."

Even Roger Staubach, the ever-present shadow, was impressed by the way Danny handled everything.

"With the weight that was on him nobody could have done a better job than he has," Roger said. "He produced immediately and that wiped out some of the comparisons right away. If he had gotten off to a shaky start, well, then he might have gotten a lot of Roger-this and Roger-that. But he made sure that wouldn't happen."

Then the next week Danny did something else to help wipe out the criticism. In a wild game with the Cardinals, the lead changed hands several times, Dallas got the ball for a final time trailing 24–20. They needed a touchdown. A field goal wouldn't help.

The Cowboys started at their 31 with just 1:52 left. Danny quickly hit Preston Pearson for fourteen yards, then went to Drew Pearson for twenty-two more. He was working coolly and efficiently, looking like you-know-who. A holding penalty put the ball back to the St. Louis 28. There were just forty-five seconds left as Danny dropped back to pass once again. Instead of going short for the first, he went for all the marbles, lobbing a high pass toward the end zone. There was Tony Hill, running under the ball to make the catch for the score. The Cowboys had done it, winning, 27–24.

"That pass is like having an ace in the hole," Danny said. "It's the same pass we tried two weeks ago at Philadelphia and it didn't work. If we had failed again people would have started talking, saying the Cowboys couldn't win in the final seconds anymore."

For the game, Danny completed 23 of 38 for 258 yards. His last-second victory was a real high point. But the following week came a low point, a 38–35 upset by the Giants, as Danny had his poorest day, throwing five interceptions to the alert Giant defense.

"There were five different reasons we lost," he said, not making any excuses, "the five interceptions. There is no way the Giants can beat us if we just play our game. This was a chamber of horrors." Tony Dorsett had run for 183 yards, but Danny didn't compliment him through the air.

A 31–21 victory over St. Louis followed. Danny bounced back with a 20 of 36 performance for 296 yards, including a 58-yard TD pass to Hill. He didn't let the bad game against the Giants bother him. This was followed by a tough, 14–10, win over Washington. Danny had another bad day, with four intercepts in his sixteen throws. The club won and was 9–3. A 51–7 laugher over Seattle was win number ten.

Danny was 14 of 26 for 159 yards and no intercepts in a 19–13 win over Oakland. But then came another disappointment, a 38–14 loss to the Rams, in which the Cowboys were shut out until the final period. Danny had another of those days. Playing from behind, he threw three more intercepts and was just nine of 23, giving way to Carano in the final minutes. For some reason, the club had lost consistency in the second half.

They came back to win a big one, 35–27, over Philly to close the season at 12–4. The Eagles were also 12–4, but won the divisional title because they had scored more total points in splitting their two meetings with the Cowboys. Still, Dallas was in the playoffs as a wild card entry. Danny closed it out with a 16 of 24 performance, good for four big touchdowns. So he finished with a flourish.

But he hadn't been quite as sharp during the second half of the season, throwing interceptions in bunches during several games. Yet he wound up his first year as a regular in fine style. Danny completed 260 of 436 passes for a 59.6 percentage and 3,287 yards. His 28 touchdown passes set a Cowboy club record, while on the other side of the coin, his 25 intercepts tied a club mark. He ended up the seventh leading passer in the NFC, the intercepts hurting his final rating.

There were still the playoffs to contend with, and in the wild card game the Cowboys went up against the Rams, the team that had beaten them badly several weeks earlier. But this game was different. It was close until the half, with Dallas leading, 16–13, but the Cowboys totally dominated the second half, winning 34–13, as Danny hit for 12 of 25 for 190 yards and three touchdowns.

The next week they had to play the Atlanta Falcons for the right to go to the NFC title game. Playing at home, the Falcons came out breathing fire. They took a 10–3 lead in the first period, highlighted by a 60-yard scoring bomb from Steve Bartkowski to Alfred Jenkins. After the Cowboys tied it on a five-yard pass from Danny to Billy Joe Dupree, Atlanta scored again to take a 17–10 halftime lead. They upped it to 24–10 in the third period and were in good shape as the final session began.

Then it looked as if the Cowboys were coming on. They drove downfield with Robert Newhouse scoring from the one. The kick made it 24–17. But the next time they had the ball, Danny made a mistake. Tom Pridemore intercepted and returned it 22 yards. Minutes later Tim Mazzetti booted a 34-yard field goal to make it 27–17. Only 6:37 remained. Things looked bleak.

But Danny and the offense didn't panic. They took the ball at their own 38 and began driving. Danny threw five straight passes, hitting on four of them. The last one was a 14-yard completion to Mr. Clutch, Drew Pearson,

for the score. Septien's kick made it 27–24. Now there
was 3:40 left.

Atlanta hoped to run out the clock, but the Dallas
defense held. The Falcons punted and the Cowboys had
it seventy yards away, at their own 30 with 1:48 left. A
field goal would tie it. Danny started pitching again. He
hit Butch Johnson for twenty yards to midfield. Then he
went to Preston Pearson for fourteen and Dorsett for
thirteen more. The ball was at the Falcon 23 with less
than a minute to go. But the Cowboys wanted to get
even closer before sending Septien on.

So Danny dropped back again. Only this time he
looked all the way and saw Drew Pearson heading into
the end zone. He fired . . . and connected! Touchdown!
With forty-two seconds left the Cowboys had scored.
The extra point was missed, but it was still 30–27, and
that's how it ended.

Danny had pulled a big game out, in the same dramat-
ic manner that another Dallas quarterback so often did.
Safety Charlie Waters called it a miracle victory, and
Danny gave credit to his receiver.

"I threw the quick post where I thought only he could
get it," Danny said. "I didn't think he would, but he
made a great catch."

It had also been a great game for Danny White. He
completed 25 of 39 passes for 322 yards and three scores,
while having only one picked off. It was possibly his best
performance under pressure since becoming a starter.
Now the Cowboys would be meeting their arch rivals,
the Eagles, in the NFC title game and a trip to the Super
Bowl.

Only it wasn't to be. In 1980, the Eagles had an aggressive, superior defense to go with a fine offense.
Though the teams had split two meetings in the regular
season, it was the Eagle defense that really dominated
the title game. They held Tony Dorsett to just 41 yards
rushing, and Danny to only 127 yards passing. That

should tell the story right there. Though the Dallas defense played well also, Philly won the game, 20–7. So it would be the Eagles who would be headed to the Super Bowl as the Cowboys headed home.

Still, no one could fault Danny White. He had stepped into a pressure-packed situation at the beginning of the year and he had done the job. He had played a major role in his team getting to within a step of the Super Bowl, and you can't ask for much better than that.

Hopefully, there would be less pressure on Danny as 1981 began. After all, he had proved himself. He was now comfortable running the team and the players knew him, what he could and would do. Yet Coach Landry said a strange thing.

"I wouldn't be too surprised if Danny's performance level falls off a bit this year," he said. "It seems to always happen that way. You come in the first time and have a great year and it's very hard to repeat it the following season."

Even Danny was puzzled by that one. "I don't know why he'd say that unless he's trying to protect me, take some of the pressure off. But I don't know why I can't keep improving. I know one thing. I'm not going to throw twenty-five interceptions again. Maybe half that much would be acceptable."

Danny started 1981 like a seasoned veteran. The Cowboys opened with the Redskins again and won easily, 25–10. Danny fired two long touchdown passes while completing 12 of 24 for 145 yards. He didn't have to throw any more because Tony Dorsett was ripping off 132 yards on the ground while Ron Springs added 58 more. The club looked strong again.

A 30–17 victory over the Cardinals followed, Danny throwing for 240 yards and Dorsett running for 129. It was always easier for the Cowboys when Dorsett got more than 100 yards. The stats prove it, and it was fine with Danny. He was more dangerous when the defense had to worry about the breakaway talents of Touchdown Tony.

Then in a Monday game with New England Danny sharpshooted 24 of 34 for 218 and two scores, while Dorsett did the rest with 162 yards. The club won, 35–21, as the ground game rolled up 237 yards, to go with Danny's 218. Perfect balance. A close, 18–10, win over the Giants followed, highlighted by a 41-yard touchdown strike from Danny to Butch Johnson. After four weeks the Cowboys were unbeaten and Danny was second to San Francisco's Joe Montana in NFC passing.

But just when things were looking rosy there was the inevitable upset, a 20–17 loss to St. Louis. After that game a disturbing statistic emerged. In five games the Cowboys had failed to score a touchdown on eleven occasions when they had the ball inside the opponent's ten-yard line. That wasn't good. Then came a meeting with the vastly improved San Francisco 49ers and everything came apart.

The 49ers' defense was all over Danny and his mates. He was sacked three times and often had to throw with defenders already pulling at him. Dorsett got just twenty-one yards on nine carries. Meanwhile the 49ers' offense behind Joe Montana rolled over the Doomsday Defense. The final was 45–14, a devastating defeat. Danny was just eight of 16 for 60 yards and gave way to Glenn Carano midway through the second half.

"We ate humble pie," was the way Dorsett put it. Now the Cowboys trailed the 6–0 Eagles by two full games in the NFC East. In addition, Danny had dropped to fourth in the quarterback rankings and had thrown just six TD passes in six games, with four intercepts. Maybe Coach Landry was right. His performance was going to fall off.

The club righted itself, however, against the Rams. They beat L.A., 29–17, with Dorsett rebounding for 159

yards and Danny coming up big with 277 yards, including a 63-yard TD toss to Tony Hill, the longest of his
career. The club had to find consistency because they
were headed into a tough stretch of games. Another consolation was that the Eagles had lost, bringing the Cowboys within a game of the top.

Miami was the first of those tough games, and this
was a beauty. It was close all the way, with the Cowboys
leading by a 14–13 count after three periods. Danny had
gotten one of the scores on a 21-yard pass to Johnson.
Then came the hectic fourth period.

A pair of Miami touchdowns gave the Dolphins a
27–14 lead. It was time for a patented Cowboy comeback, and at this point they really needed it. Starting
from the 21, Danny drove the club seventy-nine yards,
passing to Doug Cosbie for the score that made it 27–21,
with just 3:48 left. Miami received the kickoff, but two
plays later safety Dennis Thurman intercepted a pass
and took it to the Miami 12.

Danny wasted no time. On the first play he dropped
back, surveyed the field, and coolly tossed a scoring pass
to Ron Springs, who had beaten his defender down the
right side. The kick made it 28–27, and the defense did
the rest. So the Cowboys had another last-minute victory with Danny the engineer. He had completed 22
of 32 passes for a career high 354 yards and three
touchdowns.

The following week they did it again. It was a head-to-
head meeting with the Eagles and a chance to tie for first
place. For three periods the Philly defense was doing it
again. The Eagles led, 14–3. Then early in the fourth period Danny drove the club seventy-five yards and hit
Doug Cosbie for the touchdown from the 17. Midway
through the session they got the ball at the Eagles 39 and
went again, with Dorsett slashing the final nine yards for
the score. The score was 17–14, and the defense held
Philly until the gun.

"The character of this team shows in that we really come out fighting when our backs are against the wall," said Danny, who was 13 of 24 for 203 yards. "It's easy to crawl into a hole and say, 'Forget it.' But we play our best football when we're behind. We get fired up."

Someone else who was happy to see Danny bringing the club back like that was none other than Roger Staubach.

"Coming from behind is a Dallas tradition," he said, "that goes all the way back to Don Meredith. You have to believe in the guy who is in the middle of it. Dallas still has all the big play people like Tony Hill and Tony Dorsett, and it didn't take them too long at all to develop the same confidence in Danny that they had in me."

Staubach also talked again about how they differed as quarterbacks.

"I usually waited and threw the pass a little harder," he said. "Danny throws a little more on anticipation. This is not to say Danny doesn't have a strong arm. In fact, I think his arm strength is a little underestimated."

Danny was still high during the week following the Philadelphia game. He praised his offensive line for giving him flawless protection. He loved to win them that way.

"There's no high like throwing a touchdown pass in a big game," he said. "There's just no feeling quite like it. But things can also go the other way very easily. You take your chances out there. The highs are tremendously high, and the lows are just as low."

Danny was to experience both the next two weeks, a high with a 27–14 Monday night win over Buffalo, and a low the following week when the Lions edged the Cowboys, 27–24, coming from behind to do it. But Danny's 20 of 30 performance put him back atop the NFC quarterback ratings.

Next the Redskins fell, 24–10, then the Bears, 10–9.

But in that game Danny was knocked out of action with a cracked rib. Glen Carano came on to throw for 131 yards and help pull the game out. Carano played the next week in a 37–13 win over the lowly Colts, Dorsett doing most of the damage with 175 yards. Danny must have known how Carano felt, getting his first real action in five years.

But the next week he was back, leading the Cowboys over the rival Eagles, 21–10, throwing for 264 yards on 17 for 30, two touchdowns, no intercepts. After fifteen games he still led the NFC in passing.

It was then that someone pointed out an interesting fact. Though Staubach had retired as the NFL's all-time leading passer, had led the league several times, had played in five pro bowls, he was never named the All-pro quarterback on any of the three all-star teams considered as all-pro squads. Roger attributed that to the Cowboys winning ways.

"Dallas has always been a winning team," he said, "and it seemed that in years when I was considered to have been in the running for all-pro, some team would come out of the woodwork and the guy quarterbacking that team would be the all-pro."

The reason it came up was that the Pro Bowl squads had already been named, with Joe Montana and Steve Bartkowski as the NFC quarterbacks. Roger and many other people felt Danny deserved to be there.

"Danny will have a lot of pro Bowls," Staubach said. "But this is one he'll just have to look back on, and everybody will know he deserved it, anyway. He and Montana are the two premier quarterbacks in the NFC this year. Not having Danny there kind of takes away the credibility of the team."

As for Danny, he admitted that not being picked bothered him a bit.

"I was a bit disappointed," he said, "but thinking back, I'm happy for the guys on our club who made it.

It wasn't anything devastating to me. Besides, I feel good about the way things have gone this season.

"I feel I'm doing things better, like reading defenses, finding the open receiver, and not throwing as many interceptions. Plus it's been a different kind of year offensively because the running game is so strong. We haven't had to rely on passing as much. Last year all the big plays came on the passing game. This year we have more of a ball-control offense.

"So statistically, maybe I haven't had any great, great games, but I haven't had bad games, either."

Dallas lost its final game to a scrappy New York Giants team that had to win to make the playoffs. The Cowboys were already NFC East champs. The score was 13–10, in overtime, as Danny was 17 of 33 for 200 yards, a touchdown and an intercept. The club finished at 12–4 to top the Eagles by two games.

In his second full year, Danny had completed 223 of 391 passes for 3,098 yards and a 57.0 completion percentage. Those figures were all down slightly from the year before, but there was more running. He threw for twenty-two touchdowns, and cut the intercepts to thirteen. Joe Montana had edged him for NFC passing honors in the final week, but he was a strong second. He also had another fine year punting, continuing to do double-duty in that department.

Dorsett also had his finest year, gaining 1,646 yards on 342 carries and losing the rushing battle to rookie George Rogers by twenty-eight yards. Rogers carried the ball thirty-six more times. Ironically, the Cowboys did not have a single receiver among the top eighteen in the NFC in passes caught. That's how much Danny spread things out.

Now it was on to the playoffs once more. As Danny had said when someone asked him about not making the Pro Bowl:

"There's only one bowl game I want to win."

That, of course, was the Super Bowl. To get there, the

Cowboys first had to play the wild card Tampa Bay Buccaneers. It was a laugher. The defense was sharp as nails, while Danny and his runners did the rest. Dallas won, 38–0, and now moved into the NFC title game against one of the surprise teams of the year, the 49ers, who had given the Cowboys a thrashing early in the season.

This one was a ballgame. The crowd at Candlestick Park was rooting the 49ers home, but the Cowboys were giving them all they could handle. San Francisco scored first on a short pass from Joe Montana to Freddie Solomon. Still in the first period Septien booted a 44-yard field goal to make it 7–3. Then minutes later Danny drove the Cowboys into 49ers' territory and hit Tony Hill for a score from twenty-six yards out. The kick made it 10–7 after one. Both teams scored a touchdown in the second period, so the Cowboys held a 17–14 lead at the half.

In the third period the 49ers jumped on top with their third touchdown, making it 21–14. But then in the final session the Cowboys went to work. First Septien booted a 22-yard field goal to make it 21–20. Then midway through the period, Danny drove the club into 49ers' turf again, and this time tossed a strike to tight end Doug Cosbie from 21 yards out for the go-ahead score. The kick made it 27–21, and it looked like another come-from-behind victory and a trip to the Super Bowl.

But the young 49ers wouldn't quit. Their quarterback, Joe Montana, spearheaded an 89-yard march, and culminated it with an off-balance, third-down clutch pass to Dwight Clark in the end zone from six yards out. Ray Wersching's kick gave the 49ers a 28–27 lead. Danny had one last chance to perform a miracle of his own, but a blind-side sack by Lawrence Pillers caused him to fumble and S.F. recovered. They held on to win the game.

No one could fault Danny, or any of the Cowboys for that matter. They had played well, but the 49ers were

1981's team of destiny, going on to win the Super Bowl from Cincinnati. Danny finished the game with 16 of 24 passes for 173 yards and two scores.

Still, losing to the 49ers was a bitter disappointment to both Danny and his teammates.

"We just could never get our passing game going," said Danny, afterward, shouldering a great deal of the blame. "You need to get a rhythm going where you are moving the linebackers and secondary around, and we could never do that. So we went to the running game, which carried us much of the year. But it's a terribly frustrating feeling to come up one point short.

"On that last play I was trying to throw to a running back and I thought my arm was moving forward. Then it should have been ruled incomplete and not a fumble. But I've said before that there are both high and low points in professional football and you have to live with them. This is the lowest of the lows. I would rather have been beaten by four touchdowns than by one point."

Despite the final defeat it had been a great year for Danny White. In fact, both his seasons as a starter have surpassed most expectations. He went from four years on the bench to one of the top quarterbacks in pro football immediately. There was no transitional period. Danny had waited patiently for Roger Staubach to retire, and when he finally got the call he was ready. Those in the know feel the future is going to be even brighter.

"Danny has such great poise and such a grasp of what's going on out there," said Coach Landry. "He's a winner and as far as I'm concerned the best quarterback in the conference. If he has the same supporting cast that Roger had for ten years he should end up with comparable stats."

And that man Roger, whose name will always be linked with Danny's, also felt his successor was well on his way.

"If I was starting a team right now I would put Danny

White in there as my starting quarterback," he said. "It won't be very long before he is the premier quarterback in the league."

But it wasn't a cakewalk. Counting two years in the World Football League, it took seven years from the time he graduated from Arizona State until Danny got a chance to quarterback an NFL team. Looking at him now, it's a certainty that he could have done it a lot sooner. One person who always believed was his father, "Whizzer" White. And when he said the following about his son, Mr. White was really describing the character of Danny White, the strong stuff of which he is made.

"I know how hard it was for Danny," Mr. White said. "When he was sitting all those years just waiting for his chance I would often call him from Mesa just to talk about something besides football. But I never had any doubts he would make it, not from the time he was a little kid.

"He was always so determined. When he was eight or nine, I would take him hunting with me. We would often walk for miles and I knew he was getting tired. But he would never let me carry him until I'd say, 'Well, I need you on one arm to balance my gun on the other.' Then he'd say, 'Okay, Dad, if it will help you.' "

It's like that now with the Cowboys. Danny White is right there to give them balance and help. And he does it exceedingly well.

JOE THEISMANN

There was a time, not so long ago, when a reporter asked the Washington Redskins' Joe Theismann to list the qualities of a good NFL quarterback. After thinking a few seconds, the veteran signal-caller said:

"You have to start by being in good physical condition. Then, of course, you need a good arm and a good head. You also have to completely understand your own offense and be able to read defenses. But the toughest thing I had to learn was that the quarterback is only one-eleventh of the offense. You've got to let your teammates do their thing instead of always trying to make the big plays yourself."

In some ways, that is a startling admission for an NFL quarterback, especially one who has always been filled with an abundance of self-confidence. After all, it's always easy to find a scapegoat instead of blaming yourself. But self confident as he is, Joe Theismann is mature enough to know he hasn't always played under control, and now can see clearly some of the reasons why certain things have happened in his past.

Perhaps it was Joe's self-confidence that often made him feel he could do it by himself, that his performance would control the outcome of the game. In fact, that was often the case. Then, too, he had always met with success and suffered few setbacks before he entered the National Football League.

That entrance itself was delayed for several years. After completing a record-breaking career at Notre Dame, Joe opted for Canadian football, and starred for three seasons with the Toronto Argonauts of the CFL. When he finally decided to return home, he figured he'd win the starting job with the Redskins within a relatively short time. But it took five frustrating seasons for Joe to finally emerge as number one, and another year for him to attain the stardom he always felt would be his.

Along the way, there were many obstacles. For years, he had to prove that he wasn't too small, first for big time college football, then for the pros. It was a rap made more real by the fact that he was only a fourth round draft choice in 1971, the 99th player and eighth quarterback tabbed that year by the NFL. This came after he had finished second in the Heisman Trophy balloting his senior year at Notre Dame, and was one of the big reasons he turned to Canada. He also had to show that a mobile, so-called scrambling quarterback could fit in with a conservative system, where the QBs had been standard, dropback passers for years. In addition, he had to prove himself a leader to a team of veterans, many of whom looked upon him as a cocky kid who often mouthed off and did little else.

So for a few years it was extremely difficult for Joe to keep things in perspective. He was in a situation faced by many star athletes, who, for the first time in their sporting lives, found things not going their way, the action revolving around someone else. It was like being put on the back burner. Joe didn't like it and looked desperately for a way to do something about it.

Joe Theismann was born on September 9, 1949, in New Brunswick, New Jersey. His parents were both hard-working folks. His father, also named Joe, owned his own service station in South River, New Jersey, for a time, and his mother worked at the national head-quarters of the Boy Scouts of America in New Bruns-wick.

Young Joe took to sports early. Baseball was his first love, then basketball. He was always small for his age. In fact, that was the reason his mother wouldn't allow him to play Pop Warner football when he was still a kid.

"My mother didn't let me play football until I was twelve," said Joe. "She was always afraid I'd get hurt."

But he was already playing a lot of baseball. By the time he was a Little Leaguer shortstop at the age of nine, he was a star and considered brash and cocky, and something of a hot dog. Then, when he was twelve, Joe began playing football. He immediately began compet-ing with older boys, some of them years older, which can be a big difference at that age. As usual, he did well.

By the time he entered South River High School he was a fine all-around athlete and also an excellent stu-dent. He had a strong arm and obvious leadership quali-ties, so despite his small size, he became a quarterback and by the end of his sophomore year he knew he wanted to continue with football. He looked forward to a big junior year, hoping to attract college recruiters to South River High. But in September came an unex-pected setback, an injury unrelated to the dangerous game of football.

Joe went swimming with some of his friends and did something very foolish. "I dove into a foot of water," he said. The result was a dislocated left shoulder. As Joe recalled, "The doctor popped it back in, but he said I'd need an operation if I was going to continue with foot-ball."

The operation was to tighten the shoulder so it wouldn't pop out again when Joe was hit, something

that could make the dislocation chronic. It kept him out
for all but the final three games of his junior year, a big
disappointment. Yet despite the injury, and despite the
fact that he was barely six feet tall and weighed in the
neighborhood of 150 lbs., he was beginning to attract
attention.

Joe's talents, by this time, were obvious. Though
small in stature, he nevertheless had a major league arm
and was extremely quick on his feet. Charging linemen
rarely got a clean shot at him, and once he scrambled
out of the backfield he ran with the verve and dash of a
top halfback. He also had the ability to pick out open
receivers and deliver the ball quickly. He was without a
doubt, a winner.

Completely healthy for his senior year, he really
began hanging up the numbers as well as the victories.
He had a fine team around him and South River quickly
began attracting attention, as well as a slew of college
recruiters. By then, Joe knew he wanted to play big-time
college football, and with his ongoing sense of confidence, was even thinking beyond that to pro ball.

He was beginning to hear the sales pitch from a multitude of college recruiters and would soon have to make
a decision that is very difficult for high school stars.
Though he still didn't know where he would go in the
fall of 1967, Joe knew one thing about his future.

"Wherever I go," he said, on more than one occasion,
"I want to make sure that I play and don't sit on the
bench."

Even then he hated sitting. He wanted to be in the
thick of the action, as he was week after week at South
River High. While many schools were interested, there
was still the persistent question about his size. One of
those who wasn't sure was Peter Lusardi, then the top
recruiter in the New Jersey area for Notre Dame University.

Despite Joe's success and the raves of others who saw him, Lusardi's first notation was a terse *too small*. Finally, though, the recruiter sent one of his aides to watch Joe again, and the man returned with the information that Joe seemed ready to sign a letter of intent to attend North Carolina State. This bit of information made Lusardi more interested and he went to meet Joe himself. He then sent films of Joe's play to Notre Dame so they could be viewed by Irish coach Ara Parseghian. Parseghian was apparently impressed by Joe's quick release, as well as his speed and agility. He asked Lusardi to make every effort to sign the youngster.

Finally Joe did visit the Notre Dame campus and spoke directly with Coach Parseghian. He knew the chances of stepping into a starting role as a sophomore wouldn't be good, since the Irish had an outstanding quarterback in Terry Hanratty, who would be a senior that year. But he was impressed with the school, its academic and athletic program, and with Coach Parseghian. But it took a story in a local New Jersey newspaper to push him over the top.

The story claimed that Joe was just 5–10 and weighed 148 lbs., and said that he would "get killed," if he tried playing football at Notre Dame. This served to stoke the competitive fires that burned within this intense young man. He didn't like anyone saying he couldn't do something, or predicting he wouldn't be successful at it.

"I think that story really did it," Joe said. "Of course, I also chose Notre Dame because of the athletic and academic competition. I had no plans to leave South Bend without a degree. And I was also thinking about possibly playing pro ball someday. I felt going to Notre Dame would help me achieve that if I chose."

So in the fall of 1967 Joe became part of the Fighting Irish tradition, one that was already filled with legendary names: Rockne, Gipp, the Four Horsemen, Leahy,

Hornung, and Ara Parseghian. There wasn't a school in the land with more prestige or one where the spotlight would shine any brighter on a young star.

Though full of confidence, Joe also knew he couldn't waltz into Notre Dame and claim the quarterback job, or even that of heir apparent. He would have to work. He learned there would be some nine other quarterback hopefuls coming to South Bend, and logic told him most, or maybe all of them would be taller and heavier, would look more like a big time college quarterback. So to get a leg up on them, he reported a week early and worked directly with the coaches to learn the Notre Dame system. By the time the other candidates arrived, the coaches were using Joe to demonstrate the plays. He had made a fast start.

There was soon little doubt that Joe was the class QB of the freshman team. He did everything asked of him and showed he could handle whatever pounding his opponents handed out. He was still thin, but tough and wiry, and his great quickness often got him out of trouble and avoided many of the bone crunching collisions. By the time 1968 rolled around, Joe was penciled in as the number two man behind senior Hanratty.

Of course, that was no guarantee that Joe was going to see action. Hanratty was an all-American, a potential Heisman Trophy winner, and along with end Jim Seymour, was already carving his own niche in Irish passing annals. So Joe was well aware that unless Hanratty was hurt or fell into an unexpected slump, he probably wouldn't see much action. But he was willing to wait, because with Hanratty graduating he felt the next two years would be his.

There was someone else on the Notre Dame campus who was already thinking ahead, anticipating a Joe Theismann era. He was Sports Information Director Roger Valdiserri, who took a liking to Joe immediately.

"Joe was an energetic, hard-working guy," said Valdiserri. "You could see he was special, very mature for his age. He had 'winner' written all over him."

With an eye toward the future, Roger Valdiserri asked Joe how he pronounced his last name, Joe replied that the family always pronounced it THEESman. Valdiserri shook his head. From now on, he told Joe, it would be pronounced ThEYESman. When Joe asked why, Valdiserri replied quickly:

"It's simple, Joe," he said. "Theismann, as in Heisman."

He wanted Joe's name to rhyme with that of the trophy given annually to the best college player in the land. It could be a promotional coup. If the time came when Joe was in the running for the trophy, the association would be a natural. Heisman . . . as in Theismann.

But that was just some early insurance for the future. Now, the 1968 season was beginning and the Fighting Irish had another powerful team, one that could very well be in the running for a national title. They would have a tough nut to crack in the opener, meeting the mighty Sooners of Oklahoma.

Oklahoma took the early lead at 14–7, but after that it was all Irish. With Hanratty and Seymour looking extremely sharp in the opener, Notre Dame controlled the play in the second half and won easily, 45–21. There was no question about the Irish offense. It was in good hands. Joe would have to wait his turn.

A week later any dreams of a national title pretty well disappeared. Notre Dame played a powerful Purdue team, led by quarterback Mike Phipps and versatile halfback Leroy Keyes. The Boilermakers exposed some Irish defensive weaknesses and won big, 37–22. Hanratty threw the ball forty-three times in a losing effort, but he proved once more that he was one of the top passers in the country.

The next three weeks the Irish rolled, whipping Iowa, Northwestern, and Illinois by lopsided margins. In these games Hanratty continued to stand out, as he surpassed the legendary George Gipp in career total offense for Notre Dame. It was also in these games that Joe saw his first varsity action. He was just mopping up, but it was a good way for him to break in.

He quickly showed the same qualities that had been in evidence at South River High. He was extremely quick, could run when he had to, and threw with patience and accuracy. There seemed to be little doubt that he was being groomed as the Irish quarterback of the future.

Then came another setback. The Irish were beaten by archrival Michigan State, 21–17, dropping their record to 4–2. An easy 45–14 victory over Navy followed, then the club went back to work, preparing to meet the University of Pittsburgh, another game they figured to win easily. But during the week something happened that might possibly change the direction of the entire season.

During a morning practice session Hanratty went down. He was helped off the field, favoring a knee. The word spread quickly across the Notre Dame campus, and everybody kept their fingers crossed, hoping the injury wasn't serious and that their all-American quarterback would be ready Saturday. But it wasn't long before the verdict came. The injury was serious. Hanratty was not only out of the Pittsburgh game; he was finished for the season. With three games still remaining, including the season ending battle with powerful Southern Cal, the quarterbacking mantle had been put on the slim shoulders of young Joe Theismann.

Perhaps it was the Notre Dame's own campus football publication that best voiced everyone's concern about the change of command.

"With Hanratty out," it said, "the quarterbacking responsibilities fell to sophomore Joe Theismann, a fourth-quarter substitute for Hanratty in previous games. In his few appearances, Theismann had looked good, showing fine running ability and sharp execution of the plays. Still, many wondered if he could completely fill the breach left by Hanratty. While Hanratty weighs well over 200 lbs., and owns most of the ND passing records, Theismann is a light 160 lbs. and has attempted only eleven passes all season. If Notre Dame is to remain in contention for a high national ranking, Theismann would have to keep from being injured by giant linemen and also supplement the powerful Irish running attack with accurate passing."

So there it was again. The question of size and durability. The only way Joe would beat the rap was to go out and do it. His concern, of course, wasn't his size or toughness. It had never been. He was concerned about his lack of experience running the Irish offense.

"I felt the Pittsburgh game would be a really big test of my passing," Joe said. "Other than that, however, I wasn't too worried."

It was a cold, wet day at South Bend as the Irish prepared to do battle against the visiting Panthers, not the kind of weather for a young quarterback to debut. But Joe had a veteran team around him and he quickly went to work. The Irish got the ball for the first time on the Pitt 45-yard line and four plays later Joe had them in the end zone, halfback Bob Gladieux carrying over for the score.

The next time Joe came on he started at his own 33. This time he guided the Irish 67 yards in 11 plays, scoring himself on a ten-yard quarterback keeper. During that drive he connected on several passes, including two beautiful throws to the all-American Seymour, covering 20 and 29 yards. The Irish had gone to their sophomore quarterback without seeming to lose any firepower at all.

"That second drive really helped my confidence," Joe said, "especially with my longer passes. Of course, it's easy with a receiver like Jim Seymour. He can make any pass look like a well-thrown ball."

From there the rout was on. Midway through the second period Notre Dame had run it up to 43–0 and Coach Parseghian began to empty his bench. Things slowed in the second half, but the Irish won a lopsided, 56–7, decision. Admittedly, it was a weak Pitt team and Joe hadn't really been tested. But on the other hand the game allowed him to get the feel of running the offense without any real pressure.

The problem was that the next game would be more of the same. The Irish met Georgia Tech on another rainy, muddy day. Despite the field conditions, Joe passed and ran very well and had the game in the bag by halftime. The final was 34–7. Now there was just one game left. Only this one would be different. There would be pressure, a great deal of pressure, on Joe. For Notre Dame would be meeting the unbeaten and top-ranked USC Trojans, a club that featured running back O.J. Simpson, the most electrifying college performer of the year. Add to that the fact that the game would be played at Southern Cal and no one gave the Irish much of a chance.

There were some 85,000 fans at the Los Angeles Coliseum, almost all of them there to watch the Trojans wrap up another national title. Notre Dame received the opening kickoff. After a running play brought the ball to the 16-yard line, Joe dropped back to pass, looking for Jim Seymour. He tossed the ball out into the flat where Seymour was waiting. But at the last second USC defensive back Sandy Durko stepped in front of Seymour, picked the ball off, and rambled untouched twenty-one yards for a score.

Just forty seconds had elapsed and USC was on the board, and as Joe walked slowly to the sideline, Irish fans had to be wondering if the early intercept would destroy the young quarterback's confidence. But as Coach Parseghian approached Joe to console him, the QB looked at his coach and said:

"Don't worry, we'll get it back."

It was an incredible show of confidence for the sophomore in his first big game. But Joe was true to his word. He brought the offense out after the ensuing kick-off and promptly put together a sustained, ball-control drive. The line was opening holes for the runners and Joe went right back to the air without trepidation. The drive resulted in the tying touchdown. And before the first half was over, the Irish had scored twice more to astound everyone with a 21–7 lead.

Joe was playing brilliantly. On one of the drives with the ball on the Trojan 13, he pitched out to halfback Coley O'Brien, a former quarterback, who began running wide, then suddenly pulled up and fired a pass toward the end zone. The man there to catch it for a score was none other than number 7, Joe Theismann. It really looked like an Irish day, especially with the defense also playing well and bottling up the elusive Simpson.

In the second half the Trojans battled back behind their quarterback, gutty Steve Sogge. They scored once with the help of a controversial pass interference penalty, and finally drove in again for the tying touchdown. Joe continued to play well, twice getting the Irish within field goal range only to have the kicker miss. When the game ended, it was a 21–21 tie, but certainly a moral victory for Joe and his teammates.

"Joe showed remarkable poise after that first interception," said Coach Parseghian, afterwards. "He could have let it affect his play the rest of the game but he didn't. He just went back out there and played like a pro."

The stats backed that up. Against the powerful Trojan defense, Joe completed 10 of 16 passes for 152 yards, yet he wasn't happy.

"We should have won it," he kept saying. "We had them beaten and let it slip away."

Joe's desire and will to win were always evident. Winning was the bottom line and there was no way to get around it. If you didn't win, you lost . . . period. Later, he would explain how he felt and why.

"I just hate failure," he said. "That's why I think all sports, and especially football, are a great way for kids to grow up. With sports, you have goals to strive for. Football was the best thing that ever happened to me because I was a rebel as a kid, hated to study, and sometimes got in trouble.

"But football taught me winning. I never bought that stuff about learning something from a loss. You learn that you get yourself upset."

So the Irish completed a 7–2–1 season and Joe Theismann proved to himself and everybody else that he was ready for big time college ball, skinny or not. For the season he had completed 27 of 49 passes for 451 yards and a pair of scores. His completion percentage was 55.1, and although he had five passes picked off, he had done well. Passing was not the only thing he did. He had also used his legs, running 59 times for 259 yards and scoring four touchdowns. By contrast, Hanratty ran just 56 times while seeing much more action. It was obvious that Joe's speed and agility would give the offense a new dimension in the years to come.

In the spring of 1969 something also happened that would greatly affect Joe's future. He heard that Sports Information Director Roger Valdiserri had a good looking new secretary. Joe decided to investigate and went to the SID office to get a publicity photo of himself for a fan. Once he met Cheryl Brown, he continued to go back every day, each time asking for another photo of himself. Finally, after several weeks of this, Cheryl told him she couldn't believe he had so many fans.

Eventually, they began seeing each other regularly, and were married at the end of the 1970 football season. Today, Cheryl and Joe have three children and his family has always been a big part of Joe Theismann's life.

The Irish had many returning lettermen for the 1969 season and some fine new players as well. So it figured to be another powerful Irish team. Just how powerful, only time would tell. There were some soft spots on the schedule, but also several big games. Joe, of course, quickly nailed down the starting quarterback spot and with Jim Seymour graduated, he would have a new primary receiver in split end Tom Gatewood.

Game one was at South Bend with the Northwestern Wildcats. When Northwestern drove into Irish territory with the opening kickoff, then took the early lead on a field goal, no one was particularly worried. After all, once the Irish got the ball, Joe and his teammates would go to work.

After two running plays gained short yardage, Joe dropped back to throw his first pass of the year. He completed it, all right, only the receiver was Northwestern safety Rich Telander, who returned the intercept all the way to the Notre Dame 14. Shades of Southern Cal from a year earlier. Three plays later the Wildcats had a touchdown and the extra point gave them an early, 10–0, lead. Irish fans were stunned to silence.

But as usual Joe kept his cool. Minutes later he led his club on a drive and took it over himself from five yards out. And before the quarter ended he brought the Irish to the Wildcat 18, then watched halfback Ed Ziegler run it in. Notre Dame had quickly regained the lead at 14–10.

The middle quarters were scoreless, as both teams made a number of mistakes. Joe wasn't having a real good day. He fumbled once and was intercepted three times. But in the final session the overall Notre Dame power prevailed. The Irish scored three more times, once on a punt return and twice on short runs by fullback Bill Barz. The final was 35–10, but coming up was a rugged Purdue team that always seemed to give the Irish fits.

Boilermaker quarterback Mike Phipps had played very well against Notre Dame the two previous years, and 1969 was not to be an exception. One statistic told most of the story. Purdue had nineteen third down situations during the game, and Phipps got them the first down on twelve of those occasions. He also got his club on the board first with a 37-yard touchdown pass in the first quarter.

Then midway through the second period, Phipps led his club on a 63-yard scoring drive that made it a 14–0 game. It didn't look good for the Irish, and for the second straight week, Joe was not playing well. He finally got things moving after the second Purdue score, engineering a 79-yard drive, which was aided by a pass interference call. He then hit Ziegler from the 10 for his first TD pass of the year. So it was a 14–7 game at half.

Purdue made it a 21–7 game in the third, then upped it to 28–7 early in the final stanza. Late in the game Joe hit Gatewood from twenty yards out for another Irish score, but that was all. Purdue won it, 28–14, with Phipps hitting on 12 of 20 passes for 213 yards. By contrast, Joe completed just four of 12 for a net of seven yards, certainly not an impressive game. In fact, there had to be those wondering whether Joe would be able to fill Hanratty's shoes or not. Maybe they would find out the following week when the Irish met the tough Spartans of Michigan State.

Joe himself was well aware of what was happening. He admitted his feelings to Coach Parseghian.

"I told him I didn't think my performance the first two games was up to par," Joe said. "The guys I was playing with were the greatest in the world but I hadn't done anything to show I was worthy of playing with them. I don't think I was tight against Purdue, though there was a lot of tension during the week. Then in the game I just wasn't accurate enough with my passing."

Parseghian, for his part, gave Joe nothing but encouragement. He still believed in the kid's ability. "I told him how I'd played with Otto Graham and even he had had off days," the coach said. "We talked about his capabilities, what he can and can't do. I told him to forget about the Purdue game and Joe responded with a great week of practice."

Against Michigan State, Joe wanted to get it going early, and he did, taking the team fifty-two yards on their second possession and capping the drive with an 11-yard TD toss to Bill Barz. Michigan State came back to tie it early in the second. Then it became a seesaw. First Notre Dame went on a long drive for a score, but the Spartans came right back with a drive of their own. Then with 2:09 remaining in the half, Joe and his teammates started from their own 27.

Now Joe really went to work, perhaps for the first time all year. After a running play gained just two, Joe kept the ball and scrambled around right end for thirteen and a first down. He then hit Barz in the flat for a 16-yard gain. Next he went to Gatewood and picked up thirteen more. That gave the Irish a first down on the Spartans' 29, with less than a minute remaining.

Again Joe wasted no time. He immediately rifled a 29-yard scoring shot to halfback Ziegler and the Irish were up, 21–14, at intermission. In the second half, Joe continued to excel. He scored himself on a seven-yard run, and after State got another, he hit Gatewood for a 23-yard TD strike. Another long drive made it 42–21 and a final Spartan score ended it at 42–28.

The Irish had won a big victory, and more important, they had their quarterback again. Joe had finally lived up to preseason expectations, producing a great game with 20 of 33 passes for 294 yards and three touchdowns. He also ran for 51 yards on ten carries. It was truly an all-American caliber performance. Michigan State coach Duffy Daugherty had nothing but praise for the young signal-caller.

"I thought Theismann had a great day," Duffy said. "I don't know how many times he came up with the big third-down play. His style of play is very effective when Notre Dame is even or leading. If you need the ball you have to come up and play his fakes on those roll-outs and options. If Notre Dame is behind, though, you can lay back and just wait for him to throw the ball. But we just weren't in that position today."

The next week it was easy, a 45–0 shutout of Army, with Joe firing a pair of TD passes to Gatewood, one of them covering fifty-five yards. The only interesting thing about the game was that it was played at Yankee Stadium in New York and Joe admitted that playing in the legendary ballpark made him nervous at the outset. But he sure didn't show it once the action started. Now it was back home for another big one, those mighty Trojans of Southern Cal.

This one was a battle. The Trojans no longer had O.J. Simpson, but were still formidable. In fact, his replacement, Clarence Davis, ran for an apparent score in the first period, but it was called back by a penalty. Meanwhile the Trojan defense was really shutting down Joe and the offense. At halftime it was still scoreless and the offense had gained just thirty-five yards.

But the Irish were fired up for the third quarter and

after taking the opening kickoff they marched seventy-four yards in eleven plays with Barz scoring from the one. That seemed to get USC pumped up, and they matched it with a 75-yard drive of their own. The game was now tied at 7–7 after three.

Then early in the fourth period the Trojans intercepted a Theismann pass and returned it to the Notre Dame 15. Two plays later they scored to take a 14–7 lead. The Irish then drove again, but with a fourth and goal at the Trojan three, Joe was sacked for a 15-yard loss. A blocked punt minutes later led to another Irish score, this one tying the game at 14–14. Time was getting short, but Notre Dame seemed to have the momentum.

They got the ball again and Joe engineered a drive to the USC 14, getting the yardage on a nifty scramble. But a controversial clipping penalty negated the gain and put the ball all the way back to the 40. They got it back to the USC 31, then lined up for a crucial field goal try. Kicker Scott Hempel booted it off Joe's hold. At first it looked like it would make it, but at the last second it dipped and hit the crossbar, rebounding back onto the field. It was no good! So the game ended in a 14–14 tie, perhaps still another moral victory for the Irish since the Trojans were rated number three in the country at the time. Joe finished the game with 11–19 for 113 yards.

Easy wins over Tulane (37–0) and Navy (47–0) followed, and then came a 49–7 swamping of Pitt and a 38–20 victory over Georgia Tech. Though the caliber of opposition wasn't all that tough, these games gave Joe a chance to pick up more valuable experience and continue to sharpen his skills. The final game was a little closer, as a lackluster Irish squad squeaked past the Air Force, 13–6. It gave Notre Dame an 8–1–1 record for a year and an invitation to play Texas in the Cotton Bowl on New Year's day.

That one would be a disappointment, though the Irish

battled the Longhorns down to the last minute. Texas won the game, 21–17, and was declared national champion. But Joe and the Irish could be proud. They came within a whisker of beating the team deemed the best in the land.

For the regular season, Joe had completed 108 of 192 passes for 1,531 yards and a 56.2 percentage. He threw for thirteen scores and had sixteen picked off. In addition, he was the team's third leading rusher with 378 yards on 116 carries for a 3.2 average. He scored six more times on the ground. It was a good year, though Joe himself wasn't satisfied. And strangely enough, the Notre Dame jury, at least among the fans, seemed to be still out when it came to Mr. Theismann.

For example, in the student-produced football review and preview, there was a story about the frosh team and players who would contribute to the varsity in 1970. In talking about the two freshmen quarterbacks, the editors mention that they "should give Joe Theismann a run for his money when practice opens next spring." And later in the article they stated: "Don't be surprised, however, if No. 7 isn't on the field when ND opens with Northwestern next year."

Not exactly a vote of confidence. Of course, the final judge would be Ara Parseghian, and Joe himself wasn't worried. He continued to play baseball in the spring and was still an outstanding shortstop and second baseman. In the spring of 1970 he batted .368 and had scouts from the Pittsburgh Pirates and L.A. Dodgers interested.

"I can't say now which sport I would pursue professionally," Joe told a reporter. "During football season I feel like I want to play in the NFL. But during the spring I forget about it and start thinking baseball. I'll just have to wait and see how my final football season turns out."

At least Joe had alternatives. He was also majoring in sociology and expected to get his degree on time, as he said he would. Despite those who still questioned his ultimate credentials, it was obvious from the beginning of practice in the fall that Joe was still Coach Parseghian's number one man. In fact, whenever someone would question Joe's ability, the coach was quick to respond. To one such question he said:

"Don't ever underestimate Joe. He can pass, he can run, he's a scrambler and he shows great leadership on the field. In other words, he's a winner. And don't let his size fool you. I know several other quarterbacks who don't have great size, such as (John) Unitas and (Len) Dawson. He can recognize defenses and he knows how to attack them. He's unpredictable—he'll gamble—and this can be a little disconcerting to an opponent. In short, he can do it all."

The Irish were looking for a great season. There appeared to be a big improvement in the defensive unit and the offense figured to be even more potent than in 1969. The line was big and strong, and Tom Gatewood was returning to catch Joe's passes. The only weakness might be the lack of a breakaway runner, though Joe's ability to motor out of the backfield somewhat made up for that.

Northwestern was the first opponent as the Irish opened on the road. Joe and his teammates showed quickly that they were ready. After the opening kickoff was run back to the 25, Joe came on and let the offense seventy-five yards in just six plays for a score. The big play was a 39-yard completion to Gatewood, and the touchdown was made on a three-yard run by halfback Denny Allan.

From there it was easy. Joe scored on a nine-yard scramble and later hit Bill Barz from the 17 with his first TD pass of the year. It was a 28–14 game at halftime with a 35–14 final, the second string playing most of the final two periods. As for Joe he was confident and executed very well. He completed just eight of 19 passes for 128 yards, but 116 yards came in the first half as the Irish got twenty-eight of their points. The ground game was devastating, chalking up 330 yards for the day. It was a solid beginning.

Purdue was next and for three straight years the Boilermakers had ended any Irish hopes for an unbeaten year in the second game. Quarterback Phipps was gone and Notre Dame was a heavy favorite, but no one expected the offensive onslaught that was to follow.

By halftime it was a 24–0 game and the final was 48–0. It was that simple, no more details necessary. The Irish offense rambled for 633 yards and Joe had a banner day. He completed 16 of 24 passes for 276 yards and three touchdowns. Gatewood was on the receiving end of all three scoring passes and in all caught twelve of Joe's aerials for 192 yards. The two were becoming quite a combination.

After the game, Purdue coach Bob DeMoss pointed to Joe's maturity as a big factor.

"Joe Theismann is the difference between Ara's team this year and last," DeMoss said.

Somebody pointed out that since Joe took over for Hanratty the final three games of his sophomore year, he had won twelve, lost just two, and tied two. And Coach Parseghian couldn't say enough about his senior signalcaller.

"Joe played extremely well," the coach said. "He had an exceptional day throwing. His leadership and direction of the team were flawless. Purdue does a fine job of using a multitude of defenses and Joe was forced to audibilize a great deal. He did an outstanding job of reading the defense. It takes a great quarterback to do that."

Others were beginning to look at Joe's abilities. For his efforts against Purdue he was named Associated Press National College Back of the Week, and he was now being looked at with some of the other fine senior quarterbacks of 1970, Jim Plunkett of Stanford, Archie

Manning of Mississippi, and Dan Pastorini of Santa Clara. And it was about this time that Roger Valdiserri really began his "Theismann for Heisman" campaign in earnest.

Next came what was expected to be another tough one, the Spartans of Michigan State. But that Irish defense was proving to be impregnable, and the offense was unstoppable. Notre Dame won easily, 29–0, with the offense racking up 513 yards. Joe was content to keep his club on the ground most of the day, as the Irish ran for 366 yards and passed for just 147. But the game showed that the Irish were contenders for the national championship and Joe Theismann was indeed a possibility for the Heisman Trophy.

In fact, by this time some reporters were asking him about it, comparing him with the likes of Plunkett, Manning, and Ohio State's Rex Kern, another fine QB.

"They're all real fine athletes," Joe said, "and I'd certainly hate to have to make the choice. My guess is the trophy will go to the man who quarterbacks the top team in the nation. If that's the case, then I wouldn't mind winning it."

The lopsided victories over Purdue and Michigan State moved Notre Dame up to third in the AP and UPI polls, trailing Ohio State and Texas. Joe was fifth in the country in total offense. He had already passed some of his Irish predecessors, such as Johnny Lujack, Paul Hornung, and John Huarte, in total offense, and if he kept up the pace he had a shot to even go past the record-holder Hanratty. But to Joe, the most important thing was winning and keeping the team unbeaten.

Army proved no real test as the Irish rolled again, 51–10, with Joe and his substitutes passing for 316 yards. Next it was Missouri, with similar results, a 24–7 Irish victory and two more TD tosses for Joe. After that Navy fell, 56–7, with Joe passing for 192 yards on 13 of 17 and the runners gaining another 408 yards. The Irish machine was simply overwhelming, and with Pittsburgh coming up next Joe was on the threshold of setting some great records.

The Panthers were a better team than in years past, coming into the game with a respectable 5–2 record. And for a short while early in the second period they looked to be making a game of it, taking a 14–13 lead and marking just the second time all year the Irish had trailed. That's when Joe went to work.

First he hit halfback Denny Allan on a 54-yard scoring pass. Next it was halfback Ed Gulyas, gathering in a 35-yard TDer from Joe. Then it was tight end Tom Creany, converting a flat pass into a 78-yard touchdown. Joe finished the day with 13 of 24 for 284 yards and the Irish had a 46–14 victory. But that wasn't all.

Joe's total offense for the day was 381 yards, giving him 4,741 for his career, and moving him past Terry Hanratty into first place on the all-time Notre Dame list. He also passed George Gipp's total career yard mark of 4,833. Joe now had 4,847, and the season wasn't over. When asked, however, he tried to discount the records.

"I was more concerned about winning today," he said. "And as far as any record is concerned, I think it should be shared as a team record, because without the rest of the guys none of it would have happened."

In the press box that day were an abundance of "Theismann for Heisman" buttons, and it was noted that this was Joe's twenty-first consecutive start. The skinny, little guy from New Jersey hadn't been hurt yet. Perhaps one reason for that was voiced by Pittsburgh linebacker Phil Sgrignoli.

"If you could get a clean shot at him you could kill him," the linebacker said. "But if you try to set him up for the clean shot he gives you the head fake or the hip and you don't get him at all. You've got to be content to just get him, and not worry about the clean shot."

After the Pitt game the unbeaten Irish were elevated to number one in both AP and UPI polls, the first time they had been in that spot all year. They expected another easy win against Georgia Tech, but it didn't happen. Though the Irish were rolling up the yards all afternoon, it seemed that either a mistake, a penalty, bad luck, or clutch play by Tech stopped their drives. At the half it was still a scoreless tie, and by the end of three, Georgia Tech was on the verge of the upset of the year, leading 7–3.

Then midway through the final period a Tech punt gave the Irish the ball on their own 20. There was a feeling that this was it. They had to go now, and Joe began moving the club. He started big, scrambling out of the pocket on the first play. It was supposed to be a pass to Gatewood, but the big end was covered. Finally Joe spotted halfback Ed Gulyas on the left side, fired a perfect pass that Gulyas turned into a 46-yard gain, bringing the ball to the Georgia Tech 34.

From there the Irish stayed mainly on the ground, with halfback Allan finally punching it over from the two. The final was 10–7 and the Irish managed to escape with their lives. Joe had thrown for more than 250 yards, but it was almost in vain.

The following week was an even closer one, a taut defensive battle with a solid Louisiana State team. This time no one scored until the final minutes of the game when Scott Hempel booted a 24-yard field goal, giving the Irish a 3–0 victory. With only Southern Cal standing between Notre Dame and an unbeaten season this was no time for the offense to go into a slump.

Before the Southern Cal game came news everyone was waiting for. It was announced that Stanford quarterback Jim Plunkett was the Heisman Trophy winner for 1970. Joe had finished a strong second, and there were still many who felt he should have won. He admitted his disappointment, but added that it was still

more important for the club to beat USC and then
hopefully go on to a return engagement against Texas in
the Cotton Bowl.

The game was played in the rain at Notre Dame Stadium and would be a contest that few people would
forget. It began like a Notre Dame day. The Irish received and started from their own 20. Joe marched the
team right up the field against the USC defense, taking
it the final twenty-five yards himself and giving the Irish
an early, 7–0, lead.

But then, without warning, the whole complexion of
the game changed, and swiftly. Led by tailback Clarence
Davis and quarterback Jimmy Jones, the Trojans
marched back down the field and tied the score. Three
minutes later they were at it again, getting another to go
on top, 14–7. When they got the ball a third time they just
repeated the pattern. This time Jones hit wide receiver
Sam Dickerson from forty-five yards out and the Trojans had scored twenty-one points in some ten minutes
to take a 21–7 first quarter lead. What's more, they did it
against a defense that hadn't yielded more than fourteen
points to an opponent all year long.

Joe threw for a nine-yard score early in the second
period, while the Trojans came back for a field goal,
making the halftime score 24–14. The Irish were still in it,
but in the third period things continued to go the Trojans' way, while the Irish were being buried by their own
mistakes.

First, a USC player fumbled on the goal line, a crucial
mistake. But the ball squirted into the end zone only to
have another Trojan fall on it for a score. Minutes later
Joe was scrambling in his own end zone when he lost his
footing in the mud. The ball squirted loose and once
again USC got it. Two fumble recoveries for touchdowns and the Trojans had a seemingly insurmountable,
38–14, lead.

It seemed like time to give up. But Joe Theismann

wouldn't quit. For the rest of the game he was a profile in courage, trying desperately to rally his team, to prevent defeat, to keep that unbeaten season from slipping away. Time and again he dropped back and threw into the teeth of a Trojan defense that knew he was coming at them. For each success, it seemed, there would be a failure.

He hit split end Larry Parker for a 46-yard TDer, as the rain and field conditions continued to worsen. But the next time he had the club moving, there was an intercept. In the fourth period he got another, bringing the club downfield and then lugging it in himself from the one. It was now 38–28.

In the waning moments Joe tried valiantly. He had two more picked off by a prevent defense that knew he was going to throw. But he still wouldn't quit, throwing to the end in one of the most courageous performances seen in South Bend in years.

The Trojans won the game, 38–28, but Joe Theismann converted still more fans. He had thrown the ball 58 times, completing 33 for the incredible total of 526 yards. To Joe, of course, the loss was all that mattered. But to others, what he had done in defeat was truly a remarkable achievement.

In fact, it had been a remarkable senior season for Joe Theismann. He had led the Irish to a fine, 9–1, record, completing 155 of 268 passes for 2,429 yards and 16 touchdowns. His completion percentage was 57.4 and he was intercepted just fourteen times. In addition, he was the Irish's third leading rusher with 384 yards on 124 carries, most carries on the club. With Tom Gatewood alone Joe connected 77 times, with Gatewood gaining 1,123 yards with those passes.

Joe's career passing stats were truly impressive. In three years he completed 290 of 509 passes for 4,411 yards, a 57.0 percentage, and 31 touchdowns. More importantly, his team won or tied all but three games he started. For a small, skinny guy who supposedly couldn't take the pounding of big time football, he didn't miss a single down due to injury.

After the end of the regular season, some very interesting things happened. For beginners, Joe was named quarterback on the Associated Press All-America team, beating out Heisman winner Plunkett and all the other so-called blue chippers in the class of 1970. He was also tabbed *Football News* Player of the Year, again over players always rated higher than he. So the respect came, ever so grudgingly.

Yet whenever people began talking about the future, about pro football, the same old, tired question arose. Was Joe Theismann big enough to play in the NFL? Reporters carried that question directly to Joe on more than one occasion.

"I think I can play," he told one. "Size is the least of my concerns. Just getting used to pro football is the big thing. It's a different kind of football."

To the same question on another day, he said: "I feel I can play pro ball because of the fellows I've played against who are now playing pro ball. It's not how big you are. It's what you have inside you that counts. If you have enough guts to give it all and you don't succeed, well, at least you haven't cheated yourself."

The bottom line was that Joe had the confidence and he now wanted the chance. He was ready to take a shot at pro ball. But he had some unfinished business first, the future engagement with Texas in the Cotton Bowl on New Year's Day. It was a typical Theismann performance. Joe controlled the game from start to finish, hitting Gatewood on a 26-yard TDer, and scoring twice himself. With a little help from the rugged Irish defense, Joe and his teammates whipped Texas, 24–11, and his college career was officially ended.

Now the draft. Like all top players, Joe had enough ego and pride to want to go high, very high. It was also good business, being a first round choice.

"Pride is just part of it," he said. "Going on the first round means most of all that a team feels you have a possibility of really breaking in quickly, and there's an excitement about having a team feel that way about you. The lower you go, the less they think your chances are and the more you've got to prove."

But there were some ill winds blowing that made it seem as if Joe might not get his wish. For instance, an official of the Chicago Bears said, "He has everything but size." A comment from the Eagles' camp was, "Joe has a lot of qualities that mark him a winner, but it would be to his advantage to have more size." And Colts' coach Don McCafferty said he thought there were four good quarterbacks available in the draft. He then named Plunkett, Manning, Pastorini, and Lynn Dickey of Kansas State. So it was hard to figure just where Joe would fit in.

On draft day there was a great deal of tension, as there is for all players waiting for the word. Finally, the roll call started. New England picked first and tabbed Jim Plunkett. Seems as if Joe was always right behind the big guy. Not this time. New Orleans had the second pick and took Archie Manning. Then came the Houston Oilers. Dan Pastorini was their man. So the first three choices of the entire NFL were quarterbacks. But none of them was Joe Theismann. Now the waiting started.

The first round ended, then the second. Still, no one called Joe. He was beginning to get upset. When the third round passed and several other quarterbacks had been picked, Joe was really beginning to sweat. It had to be the size thing. That was the only answer. Lynn Dickey went. Then Ken Anderson, at that time a little-known quarterback from tiny Augustana College. Then Leo Hart of Duke and Karl Douglas of Texas A & I. Who were they? A lot of people wanted to know.

Finally, in the middle of the fourth round the suspense ended. Joe was picked by the Miami Dolphins, the eighth quarterback and 99th player chosen. There was no way seven college quarterbacks were better than Joe Theismann.

"I was a little bit disappointed that I didn't go higher," Joe said, when the smoke had cleared. "But I wasn't dissatisfied where I went or with the team that selected me. Not the least bit."

The Miami Dolphins were an outstanding football team, perhaps one on the brink of greatness under coach Don Shula. They also had one of the fine, young quarterbacks in the game in Bob Griese, and to a guy like Joe, with a burning desire to play, that might present a problem. In fact, with Griese firmly established as number one, Joe was not certain why the Dolphins wanted him.

"Sure I'm surprised I was taken by a team with a quarterback as young as Griese," he said. "So I know at first it will be a learning process for me."

Perhaps the reason for the selection was voiced best by Dolphin player personnel chief Joe Thomas. "Joe is a great competitor," said Thomas. "He's used to playing under big time pressure and he's a Griese type, quick-footed, able to run the same type of offense Griese does. And the most impressive thing about the kid is he's a great leader. He knows how to control a football team. He's being brought in here to compete with both Griese and our other quarterback, John Stofa."

Still, it seemed very doubtful that Joe could supplant Griese. That had to be on his mind as he thought about his situation. Perhaps that was the reason that another story broke shortly after the NFL draft. It seemed that Joe was entertaining an offer from the Toronto Argonauts of the Canadian Football League.

There were a good number of American players north of the border, but the majority of them were little more than good college or semi-pro players when they headed to Canada. Most of the top players stayed home. But occasionally a CFL team would open its vaults and land a top flight American. Most times, the player would go up north for two or three years, then try to hook up with an NFL team. The desire to play against the best and at home never seemed to disappear completely.

But in Joe's case there were several factors to consider. First of all, he wasn't a first or even a second round choice of the NFL. So he couldn't really expect the big bucks offered to the top guys. The threat of a defection to Canada could cause the Dolphins to up the ante. Secondly, there was the idea of sitting the bench behind Griese. In Canada, he was probably a sure starter or at least would see considerable action.

One reason for that was the Canadian game itself. It was tailor-made for a quarterback with Joe's skills. For openers, the field is larger, being 110 yards long and 65 yards wide, compared with 100 yards long and 53 yards wide in the NFL. Plus there is a 25-yard deep end zone compared with ten yards in the American game. There are also twelve players on a side instead of eleven and just three downs to make a first instead of the American four. There are still other differences, but just these indicate a more wide-open game and the necessity for a quick, mobile quarterback who can move a team in a hurry.

The CFL was well-established, with nine solid franchises across the nation of Canada. They played in large stadiums to big, enthusiastic crowds. In other words, it was not a rinky-dink league. The Argonauts had the rights to Griese and were apparently making him a substantial offer.

"I've been up to Toronto and it's a lovely place," Joe said, in early February. "They also play an exciting brand of football. There are a lot more ways to score up there. You might say it's my type of football. Sure, I admit I'd love to prove I can play in the NFL, but there's also another way to look at it. After a couple of years in Canada maybe the United States would then believe I'm big enough to play football."

So the size thing still stuck in Joe's craw. Yet many thought he was just using the Canadian league as leverage to pry a larger offer from the Dolphins. But anyone who knew Joe also knew he was serious. He wasn't the kind of guy to play games with something like this.

The Dolphins were serious, too. Though they hadn't picked Joe until the fourth round, they still wanted him and began negotiations in earnest. At this point, Joe was working without an agent and just had his college coach, Ara Parseghian, advising him. But in early March it looked as if he was about to sign with the Dolphins.

Then on March 8, the Dolphins put out a press release saying that Joe had reached terms with the ball club. There were quotes from owner Joe Robbie, saying an agreement had been reached; from Coach Don Shula, stating that Joe would fit in with what the team was trying to accomplish; and from Joe himself, saying he was happy to reach terms on a man-to-man basis. "I'm very thankful for the opportunity to join the Dolphins," he was quoted as saying.

There was one problem. Though the parties had reached terms, there was still no signature on the dotted line. Still, the next day some newspapers had claimed Joe signed. There were more quotes from Joe on what a trying experience the negotiations had been. The story also said that Joe planned on competing for the number one job with Bob Griese.

"I don't want to come down to compete for second place," Joe said. "Even if I don't get to start, at least I'll have a great teacher."

For several weeks football fans assumed Joe had signed and would be joining the Dolphins. But in early April there was a shocking announcement from Toronto. Joe Theismann had just signed a two-year contract with the Argonauts estimated at $125,000 in salaries and bonuses, with an option for a third year. What happened to the Dolphins, everyone wanted to know?

"Joe had agreed to terms with the Dolphins," said John Bassett, the Argonauts' chairman of the board, "but when the contract was mailed to his home for signature he thought it did not accurately meet the contract as he had understood it. This gave him cause to think. He phoned us and asked if we were still interested. We were; we sent him a contract, and now that contract is signed, sealed, and delivered, and locked up in the Argos' safe."

Naturally, there was a furor. The Dolphins said they hadn't changed the contract sent to Joe. Yet word was that Joe felt the terms of his bonus had been altered in the Dolphin three-year deal that could amount to nearly $100,000. Finally Joe emerged from seclusion. He said, yes, there had been a misunderstanding in his bonus clause, but he also said the matter had been straightened out before he signed with the Argonauts.

"I changed my decision," he said, "for the security of my family and the initial guarantees involved."

So that was it. Joe Theismann would be going north and beginning his professional career in Canada. He completed his studies at Notre Dame, becoming a member of the Academic All-America team as one of the best student-athletes in the country. He graduated with a bachelor's degree in sociology. Now it was time to play ball.

Joe reported to the Argos' training camp in mid-June. Just a week or so earlier he learned he had been selected in the baseball draft by the Minnesota Twins. So his prowess on the diamond hadn't been overlooked, but by now he was totally committed to football. He would be competing for the starting job with another first-year Canadian player, Greg Barton. Barton had spent three years riding the bench for the Detroit Lions and prior to 1971 had been traded to the Philadelphia Eagles with a shot at the starting job there. But like Joe, he opted for Canada. He was considered a passer with fine potential.

"Both Joe and Greg are not merely going from college to pro ball, or in Greg's case, from one pro team to another," said Argonaut coach Leo Cahill. "They will have to adjust to a new style of game with an extra player, different defenses with the other side lining up a yard off the ball, a different field, wider and longer, and men in motion in the backfield.

"When they reach the point where they are reacting to all these things instead of thinking about them, they're on their way."

The Canadian season starts sooner than the NFL, and Joe was already playing exhibition games when the College All-Stars went up against the NFL champs from the year before. Because he had gone to Canada he wasn't eligible to play, and he had a wisp of homesickness when he read about the contest, admitting he'd like to be playing in the game.

"I know I could play in the NFL," he said. "People who say I'm too small know as much about football as I know about soccer. Coming to Canada was the toughest decision of my life and I hope I never have another one like it."

It didn't take Joe long to prove he could play the Canadian game. Sharing time with Barton in preseason, he did very well as the Argos won all four games. In his debut, for instance, he completed 10 of 20 passes for 205 yards and two scores, while Barton was seven for 20 for 84 yards. The next week Joe was six of 15 for 92, while Barton was 10 of 16 for 123. Coach Cahill couldn't really pick one over the other, and they continued to alternate, even when the regular season began.

Toronto continued to win into the regular season, with both quarterbacks contributing, though Joe seemed to have more of a penchant for the big play. In a win over Saskatchewan, Joe was nine of 15 for 158 yards. Then in the third game against Montreal, Joe really put on a show.

Deep in his own territory, he called a quarterback draw. Stepping back, he saw the hole open, then shot through. Suddenly, there was an open field and Joe turned on the speed. None of the Alouette defenders could catch him and he went 84 yards for a touchdown.

"If I got caught, I'd have felt like a fool," Joe said, later. "I always told the coaches I could do a 4.5 forty, and I figured this was the time to prove it."

Later in the game he connected on a 94-yard touchdown pass, and still later on a 78-yard completion to set up a field goal. The Argos won, 26–14, to remain unbeaten. The club continued to win and lead its division with the two quarterbacks alternating, sometimes changing on each series of downs. That's not an ideal situation for any signal caller. They like to stay in and get a feeling for the flow of the game. But with the Argos winning, no one could fault Coach Cahill's strategy. The excitement was building in Toronto because the Argos hadn't been to the Grey Cup game (the equivalent of the Super Bowl) in 21 years.

Once again Joe was proving his durability. They play rough in Canada, and on more than one occasion he was bumped around pretty good, but he continued to excel. He couldn't be intimidated and he showed again that the "too small" rap was a lot of nonsense.

The Toronto situation changed in mid-season when Barton broke the little finger on his throwing hand. That gave the job to Joe and he made the most of it. The first week playing the whole way he not only passed well, but ran for 82 yards on 11 carries. There didn't seem to be anything he couldn't do and many people were already calling him the best quarterback in Canadian football. It was hard to imagine him as a rookie.

When the regular season ended, the Argos had a 10–4 record to finish first in their division. As for Joe, he was a shoe-in for Rookie of the Year, having completed 148 of 278 passes for 2,440 yards, a 53.2 percentage, and 17 touchdowns. He also ran 81 times for 564 yards and another score. He had twenty-one passes picked off.

In the playoffs, the Argos had to play a two-game series against the Hamilton Tiger Cats. Joe led his club to a 23–8 win in the first game, then the second ended in a 17–17 tie. Since the series was decided on total points, the Argos were in the Grey Cup, and would face the Calgary Stampeders.

It was a hard-fought game in which Joe really got banged up.

"Somebody got into my face mask and hit my nose and eyes," he said. "I couldn't see right so I came out. Then I found out my nose was broken. I returned in the last two minutes and we were driving for the winning touchdown when we fumbled near their goal line."

Calgary won the game, 14–11, but getting to the Grey Cup was a big thrill for Joe. Ironically, the Miami Dolphins, which would have been his NFL team, was well on the way to the Super Bowl, which they would lose to Dallas. So Joe would have been a big winner in Miami, too, but he undoubtedly wouldn't have seen the playing time.

Coming into 1972 there was a potential problem. Neither Joe nor Greg Barton particularly wanted to alternate this time around. Joe had had a taste of being number one after Barton was hurt and he liked it.

"I'm honest enough to admit I might feel differently about Canadian football if I had to alternate with Greg for the entire 1971 season. And I really don't know how I'm going to react next season if we alternate again. Let's face it, there's a lot more incentive in competing for a whole job than half a job."

Yet it looked as if the two would be splitting duties

once more. Joe was looking sharp in the preseason. Then in the season's opener against Montreal the quarterback situation was settled again by an injury. Only this time the victim was Joe.

Early in the second half Joe scrambled and was hit by defensive end Phil Vandersea near the sideline. He stayed down and was helped from the field. The Argos were ahead, 7–0, at the time, and as Joe watched from the sideline, Montreal came back to win the game. Afterwards, Joe learned he had a fracture about five inches above the right ankle. He was to miss nine games.

Without Joe, the Argos floundered. He returned in game 11, but by then the club had a dismal, 1–9, record. He played in the final four and the club split them, to finish at 3–11. Joe hit 77 of 127 passes in his abbreviated year, for 1,157 yards and a fine, 60.6 percentage. He also threw for 10 TD's and ran for 147 yards on 21 carries, a 7.0 average. So even in four and a half games, he put together some outstanding stats.

The injury made it a disappointing year, and after it ended Joe began talking about a return to Miami in 1973. The Dolphins had become the best team in football, and in 1972 were on their way to a record-setting undefeated season, which would see them win seventeen straight, including the Super Bowl. Joe still had the option clause in his contract, but there were ways now that he could return.

The Argos' John Bassett said the club would try to bring Joe back again, but admitted that Joe "wants to test himself in the National Football League." Of course, Joe still wanted to play, not sit, and prospects at Miami dictated sitting.

"I'd say any kid who wouldn't want to play for Don Shula is out of his mind," Joe said, adding, "but there's a point where reality has to take over. I think I'm too good to sit. The opportunity to play is uppermost in my mind."

There was a great deal of talk, but by the time 1973 rolled around, Joe had decided to honor his option clause and he signed for one more year with the Argos. This time out the quarterback job was his. Barton had retired and joined the Argos front office. And when the season started Joe was his old self and the Argos were a winning football team once again.

But even as he led his club on the gridiron each week, Joe continued to talk about the future. He seemed more determined than ever to return to the NFL and prove himself. He mentioned money and security, things like that, but he had to have thought about all those people who said he was too small, and after his great career at Notre Dame, being overlooked until the fourth round of the draft.

Sometimes, he seemed to play like a man possessed. Against Montreal late in the season he was on fire, completing 25 of 37 passes for 340 yards. That's all-star work in any league. Yet in spite of his fine play most of the talk was of next year, and whether he'd return to the NFL.

Joe finished the 1973 season in fine style. He completed 157 passes in 274 tries for 2,496 yards and 13 touchdowns. His passing percentage was 57.3 and he rushed for 343 yards on 70 carries as well. The season over, the speculation began anew. But there was little secret about what Joe wanted to do. The Dolphins had won their second straight Super Bowl and had the veteran Earl Morrall playing a fine backup to Bob Griese. Yet sometimes now Joe seemed to be almost pleading to join them. One AP news release quoted him as saying:

"It may sound corny or maybe a little patriotic, but I miss America and I'd like to play with the NFL. I've apologized several times to the Dolphins. I pleaded ignorance, not innocence."

Joe was undoubtedly referring to the contract dispute of three years earlier. He wanted to bury the hatchet and start from scratch. But it was a tricky situation. If the Dolphins gave Joe a big salary or multi-year pact, based on his success in Canada, some established Miami stars might revolt. Several had already mentioned it. To them, Theismann was an untried rookie who hadn't proved anything in the NFL.

So by late January of 1974, another rumor began circulating, that the Dolphins would trade the rights to Joe. One story said they would send him to the Chicago Bears for quarterback Gary Huff and a draft choice. In addition, a new league, the World Football League, was trying to get started, and some of their representatives were in touch with Joe. It was becoming a real guessing game.

But suddenly, it was all but resolved. On January 23, a story broke, saying the Washington Redskins were talking to Joe about the possibility of his playing there. Though several other teams were interested, notably the Bears and Kansas City Chiefs, Joe had supposedly favored the Redskins. Two days later the deal was made. The Skins acquired the rights to negotiate with Joe.

It seemed like the kind of situation that could make everyone happy. The Redskins had been perennial losers throughout the 1950s and most of the 1960s. Then in 1969 the club hired the legendary Vince Lombardi as its coach, hoping he would do the same thing in Washington that he had done in Green Bay. Lombardi seemed on his way, coaching the team to a 7–5–2 finish in 1969. Then tragedy struck, Lombardi was stricken with cancer and died. In 1970, under Bill Austin, the club dipped to 6–8.

In 1971 another new coach was hired. He was the dynamic George Allen, a proven winner. Allen's credo was "the future is now," and he began stockpiling a team of veterans, trading draft choices for proven performers. He formed the Over the Hill Gang, and immediately turned the team into a playoff club with a

9–4–1 season in 1971. The next year the team was 11–3 and made it all the way to the Super Bowl before losing to unbeaten Miami. In 1973 the team again made the playoffs with a 10–4 log and they looked forward to continued success in 1974.

One thing Allen was looking for was a young quarterback. The two incumbents were both veterans. Sonny Jurgensen was 39, a picture passer, and one of the great quarterbacks in NFL history. But age and injury were taking a big toll and Sonny was due for knee surgery during the offseason. The other QB was 33-year-old Billy Kilmer, a gritty leader, who made up for a lack of natural ability with leadership qualities and a will to win that was sometimes almost unreal. After that, there was no one.

"Getting Joe was a good trade for us," Coach Allen said. "He has just enough experience to help us in 1974. He is young at 24 and the type of quarterback I've been looking for. He fits the bill better than other quarterbacks in the league and he can be brought along slowly."

And in that last phrase was a warning. Allen didn't like to use young players, preferring to stick with his vets. Joe, of course, always hated sitting. But perhaps he figured with the age of Jurgy and Kilmer, he wouldn't have to wait too long.

"I'm pretty tickled by this," Joe said. "If a contract can be worked out I think there is a better chance for me to play for the Redskins than the Dolphins. Let's face it, you don't push out Bob Griese too easily when he's in his prime."

Joe still talked of entertaining offers from the other leagues, Canada and the new World Football League, but George Allen was confident of Joe signing with the Skins. He was right. By early March the deal was set and Joe signed a three-year pact to play for Washington. He was in the National Football League . . . at last!

"This is one of the happiest days of my life," Joe said, at the signing. "My ambition has always been to play in the National Football League, and with the Redskins I have an opportunity to play with the best against the best.

"Both Sonny and Billy are great quarterbacks and I can learn a lot from them. I'm confident that I will play here, but right now all I really want to do is compete for the job and help the Redskins win the championship."

At a mini-camp in mid-March Joe looked good. He threw well and seemed to be reading defenses without too much confusion. Everybody was patting everyone else on the back and it looked like one big happy family. But when the training camps opened in the summer there was a problem. The veteran players decided to strike, and pulled out of camp.

That left just rookies and free agents to work with and it was tough. Joe felt that because he was an NFL rookie, he could report. Later, it was learned that his action angered some of the striking vets, and when they finally returned, they held somewhat of a resentful attitude toward Joe. And, as expected, when the 1974 season opened, Billy Kilmer was the Redskins' starting quarterback, with Sonny Jurgensen ready to pitch relief. Joe was third-string and relegated to the bench.

The Redskins split their first four games and were not playing consistent football. Yet Joe had seen virtually no action. It didn't surprise those who knew George Allen. The coach rarely used first-year players, especially when he had competent people ahead of them. Sitting like that was a new experience for Joe. He didn't like it, but he was trying to make the best of it.

In fact, Joe wasn't exactly sitting. He was charting plays on the sideline, working with the coaches.

"I couldn't just sit there," he said. "In fact, I haven't sat on the bench yet. That would drive me nuts. At least charting plays gives me a job to do and makes me feel

I'm contributing, plus a quarterback can learn from it."

In the preseason Joe had completed 40 of 78 passes for 463 yards, showing he could move the team and throw on an NFL level. But after four games of the regular season he had thrown just three times, completing all three. He still prepared carefully every week, just as if he would be starting. Yet he hated the inactivity on game days, claiming publicly that he was patient, that he knew he could play and that his time would come very soon, sooner than it would have at Miami. But he had to be hurting inside.

He also did not pal around with the two veteran quarterbacks, Kilmer and Jurgensen, saying there was a big generation gap between them.

"I might have learned several things from them subconsciously," he told a reporter. "But I'm Joe Theismann. I play my style of football and they play theirs. My own philosophy of how to attack a defense has been pretty successful for me up to now so I see no reasons to change something that has been working."

Soon afterward, Joe figured out a way to see more action. He did something unheard of for a pro quarterback. He volunteered to return punts if needed.

"I am a quarterback and I want to play quarterback," he said. "I certainly don't want to jeopardize my career running back punts. But I don't think I will. If Coach Allen feels it will help us get into the playoffs, I'll do it."

Sure enough, when the Skins played the Cardinals, Joe was back there with the return team. He did well, returning one eighteen yards and almost breaking it all the way. But the next week he was hit on a return and suffered a bruised thigh, keeping him out of the following game. So he was taking a risk which all the more showed his burning desire to play football.

"The key to returning punts is quickness, not speed," Joe said. "Speed is great once you get in the open field, but it's not going to always get you through that first wave of tacklers. You need quickness the first ten yards. You have to give them a leg, than take it away.''

But, as usual, whenever Joe talked football, he always came back to topic A—quarterbacking. He didn't want anyone to forget why he was really there and about the confidence he had in himself. So at the same time he talked about his punt returning, he added this:

"I'm a damned good quarterback, and although I might be doing many different things this year, like returning punts, eventually I'll be this team's offensive leader.''

Joe wasn't about to let anyone forget he was there. But his 1974 season continued the way it had started. The team made the playoffs again with a 10–4 record before losing to the L.A. Rams in the first round. Joe got into just nine of the fourteen games, completed nine of 11 passes for 145 yards and one touchdown. He also scored a touchdown on the ground, one of his three carries for twelve yards. In addition, he averaged 10.5 yards a punt return, though he didn't return that many, and he also held for field goal and extra point tries.

During the offseason there were several developments. For one thing, Joe and his family were settling into the Washington area. He bought a home in nearby Arlington, Virginia, and opened a restaurant with a couple of partners. Then he learned that Sonny Jurgensen was finally calling it quits after a brilliant career. Kilmer was still there, of course, and Allen had brought in another veteran, Randy Johnson, to make things interesting.

Joe was telling friends that he had been assured that training camp would provide him with a chance to win the regular job.

"I'm gearing myself up to compete for a starting job,'' he said. "This year I'm better prepared for it, better equipped, and I really believe I earned a chance to show what I can do.''

Joe liked to point out the final game of 1974, a 42–0, shellacking of the Bears, when he came on in the third period with a 21–0 lead and went the rest of the way. In that game he passed for one score, hit Frank Grant with a 69-yarder to set up another, and drove the club 56 yards for a third TD. In all, he completed six of seven passes for 123 yards that day and earned the cheers of a packed house at Robert F. Kennedy Stadium. It was like his whole season was wrapped up in that twenty-five minutes or so of football, and he was hoping that it would serve as a stepping stone.

During the off-season Joe worked very hard to get ready. He studied game films constantly, saying that he felt mental preparation and avoiding injuries was 85 percent of being a successful quarterback.

"I'm going after the job," he announced, confidently. "I have an edge over Randy Johnson and I think if Coach Allen is going for more movement from the quarterback I can win the job. I put in my year on the bench and now I'm ready to be a starter."

So Joe went to camp with great expectations. Then in the first preseason game disaster struck. He was in for just two plays when he dislocated his left elbow. It wasn't a serious injury, but it shelved him for the game, and the following week he was in for just eleven plays and the first pass he threw was intercepted. Meanwhile, the veteran Kilmer was having a brilliant preseason. In two games he had completed 20 of 32 passes for 250 yards and three scores. It was already pretty obvious that the job was still his if he stayed healthy. Now Joe was beginning to say publicly that he wasn't happy, that he didn't feel he was getting a fair shot.

"I don't know where I stand now," he said on one occasion. "I have pride and I feel I'm fighting for number one. Football is my way of life and I have the desire to be number one. But where I stand, I just don't know."

By the end of the preseason it was obvious that Joe simply was not playing well. Against Houston he completed just four of 17 passes and one newspaper story said: "Theismann is having more difficulties getting untracked than the U.S. economy."

Sure enough, when the season started, Kilmer was the quarterback, and the veteran was beginning to look like an ageless wonder. Billy the Kid stayed healthy and played virtually all the way. For Joe, moments of glory were indeed few and far between. Perhaps the highlight of the season came in an October game against St. Louis, when he threw for a touchdown off a fake field goal to help the Skins to a victory. Otherwise it was more of the same.

The Skins didn't even make the playoffs this time, falling short at 8–6. Joe played in all fourteen games, but threw just 22 passes, completing 10 for 96 yards. His one TD toss came off the fake field goal and he had three intercepted. It was another lost season and when it ended he was really discouraged for the first time in his pro career.

"To be perfectly honest with you," he told a Washington writer, "there was a point during the season when I considered retiring. When football leads to nowhere for me then it's time to get out. To just be a practice quarterback and spending each week emulating the other team's offenses is not my idea of playing in the NFL. I'm not asking for a job. All I'm asking for is a fair chance at a job. Period."

That's how bad the situation had become. When Coach Allen tabbed Randy Johnson the starter in a meaningless final, Joe took that to mean he wasn't really wanted.

"I don't know what my future is here," he said. "I still have another year left on my contract so right now I'm not really in control of my destiny. This year I've hardly had time to work with the offense at all. I just can't believe that in a three-hour practice there's not enough time for me to run the offense for five minutes. With that situation I haven't really had a chance to better myself as a quarterback."

There were trade rumors circulating near the end of the year and that made Joe even more unsure of his status. Yet in spite of his depression, the old confidence still managed to come through.

"I'm not going to be just a special teams player in the NFL," he quipped. "I still believe my talents are as a quarterback. I know I can play quarterback and be a damn good one."

So it was on to 1976. There was no trade, of course, and in January Joe had a talk with Coach Allen. He said he didn't want to be traded as long as the Skins still wanted him. Allen said they did.

"I love the city and the fans," Joe said. "I owe it to them to give it my best shot next year. But it would kill me to be third string again, I know that. I also know that I shot my mouth off out of frustration last year. Well, your mouth can only get you so far in life. It's time to let my performance speak."

Joe had an up and down preseason, looking good one week, shaky the next. But when he wrapped it up with a seven of ten performance against the Jets, good for 131 yards and a TD, he had at least solidified himself as the backup QB. Kilmer was still the starter, but Coach Allen acknowledged that Joe had done a fine job overall in the preseason. It was beginning to look as if his time might come after all.

Kilmer played most of the first four games as the Skins won three times. When Joe did get in, he looked more confident than in the past. But in game four Kilmer suffered a bad bruise of his right arm, and finally, after nearly three years of waiting, Joe was tabbed to make his first NFL start against the Kansas City Chiefs.

After waiting so long, he wasn't about to blow it. Joe played brilliant football, rallying the team for twenty fourth period points only to see the Chiefs win in the final seconds on a 63-yard flea-flicker play, 33–30. Blame the defense, not Joe. He completed 20 of 37 passes for 270 yards and the two touchdowns. In addition, he ran for another 38 yards, scoring once. Everyone seemed pleased, including Coach Allen who said he was leaning toward Joe as his starter the following week against Detroit. But Joe's performance might have had an even more subtle effect on the team than his stats show. One writer who had followed the team for a number of years explained:

"Maybe some members of the team had never been squarely in Theismann's corner," he said. "Maybe some had figured that his words were stronger than his actions . . . But that vanished Sunday at RFK. During that twenty-point fourth-quarter avalanche that Theismann directed, his teammates were pounding him on the back, slapping his hand, encouraging him to pull this one out."

So perhaps Joe had turned the corner. He started the next week and played well as the Skins beat the Lions, 20–7. Then he got the call again versus the Cardinals. At one point he had to leave the game with a bruised back and Kilmer went in. But Joe recovered and on the next series was told to return. Only a coaching mixup had occurred and when he reached the huddle Kilmer was already there and he unceremoniously thumbed Joe out of the game. It was an embarrassing incident and created the quarterback controversy anew.

Now it seemed a week-to-week thing. Kilmer started in a loss to the Cowboys. The next week Joe got the call and completed 20 of 32 for 302 yards and three scores in a 24–21 win over the 49ers. He certainly showed he could be an explosive force. And Joe himself said he had changed.

"Before, I was a bit of an undisciplined quarterback," Joe admitted. "I would do things just to do them instead of taking into consideration the situation or instead of remembering who does what best. Now I've learned to stay within the scheme of thinking about the offense. I know where to throw the football and I have better play selection. I'm more comfortable with the game plan now."

So the two quarterbacks alternated the remainder of the year. The Skins finished at 10–4 to make the playoffs. Joe had started five games to Kilmer's nine. The club won three of them and lost by three points or fewer in the two defeats. On the year Joe completed 79 of 163 passes for 1,036 yards, a 48.5 percentage, eight touchdowns and 10 interceptions. He also ran 17 times for 97 yards and a 5.7 average. But he certainly wasn't running as much as he had in Canada.

But when it came time for the playoffs Joe was disappointed again. Kilmer got the call and went all the way as the Skins lost to the Minnesota Vikings, 35–20. So it seemed like the same situation going into 1977, Joe vs. Kilmer, who must have seemed like Old Man River to the younger man. Joe, of course, wanted a chance to run the offense for the entire season.

Ironically, Joe had a big money offer during the spring from his old team, the Argonauts, but he wanted to stay in Washington and win the top job, though Allen had already said Kilmer was the starter coming in. The old story. Joe was also in his option year and wanted a new three-year pact as a show of good faith by the Redskins.

The 1977 season turned into almost a carbon copy of 1976, with maybe a little more leaning to Joe. Kilmer was the starter with Joe pitching relief as the season started. The club was not playing overly well, but they still managed to win three of six under Kilmer. Still, Allen wanted more zip in the offense and in game seven he went to Joe for six straight starts, and the club won four of those games.

Against Dallas in his fifth start he was 17 for 35 for 231 yards. But he had a TD toss called back by penalty, four obvious drops, and two caught barely out of bounds. The team lost, 14–7. He engineered a 10–0 win against Buffalo the next week, but then, almost inexplicably, was benched for Kilmer in the final two games, both victories. But the 9–5 record was not good for a playoff spot and Joe fumed again.

For the year, Joe was 84 of 182 for 1,097 yards and a 46.2 percentage. He had seven TDs and nine intercepts, and ran for 149 yards. It was a year quite similar to 1976. He had to have wondered if his time would ever come.

It seemed Joe was being successful at everything else he did. He had his restaurant, a part-owner in a car dealership and a long-term contract with a TV station. His engaging personality worked well on the media and he was rarely at a loss for words. He also gave a great deal of his time to charity. Yet always on his mind was the quarterbacking job.

"Nothing else means a thing unless it goes right with football," he said. "That's all I ever really wanted."

Then in January of 1978 came a shocking announcement. George Allen was fired as coach by owner Edward Bennett Williams when the two could not agree on a new contract. The new coach would be Jack Pardee, a former all-pro linebacker at Los Angeles and later under Allen at Washington. Now Joe had real hope. He knew how much Allen liked Kilmer. Pardee would be coming in with an open mind and Billy wasn't getting any younger at age 38. Joe really felt that 1978 would be the year. The league was also moving to a sixteen-game schedule, so durability would be more important than ever.

This time he was right. Joe had a great preseason, completing 41 of 76 for 455 yards and four touchdowns. What's more, he didn't throw a single interception. The quarterback job was his—finally!

The club started the year with a 16–14 win over tough New England. Then against Philadelphia the next week

Joe really showed his stuff. He hit on 14 of 29 for 226 yards, and more importantly, three touchdowns, as the Skins won again, 35–30. After that the Cardinals fell, then the Jets, 23–3. In that game Joe was a sharpshooter, hitting 21 of 30 passes and two more scores. Working with Pardee and offensive coordinator Joe Walton, Theismann was more in control of his game, staying in the pocket longer and seeing more of the field.

Then came Dallas and a big, 9–5, victory. The team was sailing with five straight victories and in first place. When they whipped Detroit the following week, 21–19, they were 6–0, having their best start in years. Joe seemed to be making everyone swallow their words. He said he could lead the team and he was doing it.

But a week later the bubble burst, the Skins losing to the Eagles, 17–10. The team played sloppy ball, but maybe they were due for a letdown. What they didn't know was it was the beginning of a disaster. A 17–6 loss to the weak Giants team followed. This shouldn't have happened. Joe hadn't played well in three weeks, beginning with the win over Detroit, and there were rumors that Coach Pardee was considering a switch to Billy Kilmer to shake things up. Joe couldn't believe it was going to happen again.

Yet against the Giants Joe had thrown three intercepts, and as one New York writer said, "He threw high, low and wide, missing open receivers time and again, and came out of the game admitting he was 'lousy with a capital L.' "

Sure enough, Kilmer got the call against San Francisco and responded with a fine game. The 39-year-old led the club to a 38–20 victory and the quarterback question began looking like a week-to-week thing again. Kilmer started two more, the team split them, then it was back to Joe. But by then the team had come apart. After a 6–0 start they finished at 8–8 and out of the money.

According to some close to the team, there were internal problems, the older players wanting Kilmer and the younger ones Theismann. By the second half of the season there were enough feuds that the club just folded.

Yet Joe had put together his best season. He completed 187 of 391 passes for 2,593 yards and 13 TDs. His completion percentage was still below fifty at 47.8, and he threw eighteen intercepts to go with the thirteen scores. But he seemed to be on the brink of breaking through.

During the off-season there were some major changes in the ball club. For one thing, Billy Kilmer finally decided to call it a career, so for the first time since he joined the Skins, Joe would be the veteran quarterback, the one whose job it was to take. Several of the other vets from George Allen's Over the Hill Gang also packed it in or were traded. The team in 1979 would have a distinct new look.

Joe had his usual busy off-season schedule, with his businesses, charity work, TV and personal appearances. But he also continued lifting weights as he had been doing the last few years. No longer was he skinny Joe, but a solid, 195-lbs. He also spent a great deal of time with Joe Walton, going over the team's offense and working to eliminate some old problems.

Though the team was supposed to be weak in 1979, they surprised everyone, and so did Joe Theismann. At long last he made good on what he had been saying since 1974, that he could be one of the very best quarterbacks in the entire league. As his tight end, Jean Fugett, said:

"We wanted Joe to have a great season without any controversy, because if he has a great season, so will we. Maybe it isn't fair, but so much depended on him. So much!"

It was the kind of position Joe wanted to be in. The team surprised everyone, staying in playoff contention right up until the final week of the season and a show-down meeting with the Dallas Cowboys. As usual, Joe was leading the team. Early on he threw for one score and ran for another, helping the Skins to a 17–0 lead. But the defense couldn't stop Dallas.

The Cowboys stormed back for three straight scores to make it 21–17. Joe wouldn't quit. He drove the team in close for a field goal, and then for two more touchdowns, giving them a 34–17 lead. Only late heroics by the Cowboys' Roger Staubach, leading his team to two scores in the final four minutes cost the Redskins the game, 35–34. They had a 10–6 season, but were out of the playoffs.

"I was empty afterwards," said Joe. "I poured my heart and soul into that game during the week of preparation. It took me a good three days before I snapped out of it. But I tell you, it showed me we were among the league's best.

"A lot of people said we'd be lucky to be a .500 team in But if you check back you'll see I said I thought we'd go 10–6 or better, and that's just what we did. Our guys were young and hungry, and had something to prove."

So did Joe. He had his greatest season by far. He completed 233 of 395 passes for 2,797 yards and 20 touchdowns. His passing percentage zoomed up to 59.0 and he was intercepted just thirteen times. In addition, he ran 46 times for 181 more yards and four additional scores. He finished the year as the second-highest-rated quarterback in the entire NFL, right behind the great Staubach. What had made the difference?

"We worked on Joe's control and his patience," said Joe Walton. "Say it's second and 12, and you have one receiver on a 14-yard route and another on a seven-yard route, Joe's inclination was to go for the man running fourteen yards deep. It never hit him that the receiver running the seven-yard route could get the first down by catching the ball and running five yards with it. That's what I mean by patience."

In 1980 there were problems. Top runner John Riggins left the club in a contract dispute. There were also injuries and problems with the once mighty defense. The club reversed itself and tumbled to 6–10, its worst finish in years. Yet Joe continued to find consistency and put together another outstanding year. He was throwing more than ever, with 262 out of 454, a 57.7 percentage, 2,962 yards, 17 scores and 16 intercepts. There was no question now that he had arrived. His goal now was to get the Redskins back on top.

Before 1981 began there was another coaching change. Pardee left and the offensive minded Joe Gibbs took his place. Riggins returned, and trades brought halfbacks Joe Washington and Terry Metcalf, both outstanding receivers as well as runners. Joe would have a fine offensive unit around him and was still the man who would have to make it all go.

The opener was a pretty good indication of what the season might be like. Going against the always-tough Cowboys, the Redskins couldn't muster a ground attack. Dallas took the early lead and Joe was forced to put the ball up often. Dallas won, 26–10, as Joe completed 22 of 48 passes for 281 yards and a score. But he was also intercepted four times by a Dallas defense that knew he'd have to throw. The Skins had a young offensive line that needed experience in a hurry, and that would not be an easy task.

Week number two confirmed many of the previous fears. Playing a young Giants team, the Skins were unable to deliver a knockout blow. Joe picked up yards through the air all afternoon, but the Giant defense, a good one, tightened when it had to. After a scoreless first half, Joe hit Ricky Thompson for a six-yard TD in the third period. But the Giants tied it and then went ahead 10–7 and finally 17–7. The clinching score came from defensive end George Martin, who scooped up a Theismann fumble and ran eight yards into the end zone.

But in losing, Joe set career highs of 27 completions (in another 48 tries) and 318 yards, yet only produced one six-pointer. He was throwing more than ever, but the offense seemed to lack balance. This time it wasn't his fault. He was the veteran and would have to wait for the young, inexperienced players to catch up.

The Cardinals handed Washington its third straight loss the next week, a 40–30 shootout, as the defense again failed to hold up its end. But once again Joe was incredible. He completed 25 of 37 passes for another career high of 388 yards and four touchdowns. Yet again his heroics were in vain. It seemed ironic that Joe had finally become the complete quarterback and now he didn't have a solid team around him.

Four weeks into the season there were four losses. Philly whipped the Skins, 36–13. Joe was 22 of 32 for 265 more yards, compared to just 150 for Philly QB Ron Jaworski. When it was over he summed things up quite neatly:

"We played toe-to-toe with them and beat them in the stats," Joe said, "but we didn't score, and when you don't do that, you don't win."

But with new players and a new coaching staff, it would take time. New coaches always put in a new system, so Joe was trying to be patient. A 30–17 loss to the 49ers tried that patience even more. Joe had an off game with 10 of 24 for 123 yards and gave way at the end to rookie QB Tom Flick. But after five weeks he had thrown for 1,375 yards, most in the NFC and second only to San Diego's Dan Fouts in the entire league. Yet what he wanted most of all was that first win.

It came the next week against the Chicago Bears. This time the club did it on the ground, Riggins gaining 126 yards and Joe Washington 88. For once, Joe didn't have to put the ball up all day and gained just 83 yards passing. But the next week it was back to losing, 13–10 to Miami despite a 17 for 23 performance by Joe. At 1–6, the season was already gone. The only thing left was to try for respectability and build a foundation for 1982.

A 24–22 win over New England followed. This time the Skins lost in the stats, but made fewer mistakes.

"Mistakes will kill you," Joe said, after throwing for 162 yards. "This time we made fewer mistakes and capitalized on theirs. And we got a bit lucky at the right time, too."

The next week the club seemed to jell. They whipped St. Louis soundly, 42–21, with Joe pinpointing 14 of 19 for 219 yards and three touchdowns, including a 38-yarder to Art Monk and a 51-yard shot to Virgil Seay. Then came a 33–31 win over a tough Detroit team, with Joe Washington gaining 144 yards and Joe hitting 19 of 31 for 287 yards. The offense was definitely becoming dangerous and explosive, and suddenly the team had won three straight and was 4–6 on the year.

Then when the club won a 30–27, sudden-death decision over the Giants, there was a feeling the season might not be shot after all. Joe had still another brilliant day, with 25 of 38 for 242 yards and two scores. But their old nemesis, the Cowboys, broke the spell with a 24–10 victory as Joe only hit on 14 of 34.

A loss to Buffalo followed, 21–14, dropping the club back to the NFC East basement at 5–8. But then the club showed that it had really developed character and an identity. First they whipped the powerful Eagles, 15–13, despite a mediocre Theismann performance. Then they trounced archrival Baltimore, 38–14, Joe hitting on 23 of 36 for 339 yards, and the next week they closed the season with an easy, 30–7, win over a very good Los Angeles team. In that one Joe was 14 of 22 for 247 yards.

The team had come from an 0–5 start to finish at .500 with an 8–8 record. And over those final eleven weeks they played just about as well as anyone in the league.

"Who knows what we might have done in the playoffs?" said Joe, happy that the club had finished so well, but disappointed that they wouldn't be going on. Yet he had put in another outstanding year.

In 1981, Joe set a team record with 293 completions in 496 attempts for 3,568 yards and a completion percentage of 59.1. He had 19 TD tosses and 20 intercepts, and was the fifth best passer in the NFC. If he hadn't had to play from behind early in the year, he undoubtedly would have had fewer intercepts and been rated even higher.

But there was little question now that the kid from South River High and Notre Dame was one of the best, a complete quarterback and outstanding team leader. It certainly took long enough, due to a combination of circumstances. Perhaps if Joe hadn't spent three years in Canada. Perhaps if he didn't have to wait four or five years for a real chance in the NFL. But that's past history. Joe Theismann isn't the kind of guy to look back. He's always looking ahead, looking to get better.

He had his first real good year in 1978, but wasn't satisfied. When it ended he went to then offensive coordinator Joe Walton and stated that he wanted to be a much better quarterback.

"I spent three weeks with Joe Walton just talking about what I needed to do," Joe said. "We took Joe Theismann and stripped him down like an automobile. We kept what we liked and made refinements on what we felt were his shortcomings."

This was after Joe had passed for more than 2,500 yards. Many quarterbacks would have looked at that stat and been content to take it from there. But for a perfectionist and workhorse like Joe, it wasn't enough.

So he continues his busy schedule, running his outside businesses, spending time with his family, and continuing to be a vary visible personality in the Washington area. He has talked about doing more TV work and maybe even trying his hand at acting. But much of that is still down the road. As a quarterback, Joe Theismann is now in his prime. He wants to lead the Redskins back to their former glory, back to the playoffs, and beyond.

So the other things will have to wait, still take a back seat to the gridiron. For as Joe has said in the past, without football, the rest would be nothing.

KEN ANDERSON

He plays his football in Cincinnati, Ohio, not New York or Los Angeles, and he likes it that way. He has been in the National Football League for more than ten years now, and is one of the highest-rated passers of all-time. Though he has won the NFL passing championship on three occasions he is rarely mentioned as one of the top quarterbacks in the league. He has often been booed by his own fans, called a robot quarterback by many, and described as dull and uninteresting by those who expect pro quarterbacks to be highly visible, flamboyant, and controversial.

National recognition has always eluded Ken Anderson during an already outstanding pro career. In fact, he often went out of his way to avoid the limelight, and to deny that professional athletes should have a special kind of mystique.

"People are always trying to make pro football players into something special," Ken once said. "But we're not. We take out the garbage and shop for groceries just like anyone else. We like to putter around the yard and talk to our neighbors. It just happens that we work on weekends, travel a little more than other people, and get a longer vacation."

But while Ken Anderson has always enjoyed a low

profile, he can no longer keep his existence a secret. For in 1981, he was part of a Cinderella story that had the entire pro football world buzzing. The two teams that made it to the Super Bowl were the Cincinnati Bengals and San Francisco 49ers, a pair of clubs with losing records the season before. The 49ers' quarterback was Joe Montana, a blond-haired, blue-eyed youngster out of Notre Dame, and his heroics were soon known all over the country.

The Bengal quarterback was Ken Anderson, still quiet and unassuming, but finally getting the recognition that had been missing for so many years. Not only was he the league's top passer once again, but he provided his young club with leadership and stability.

Yet while he was finally getting plaudits long overdue, not too many people knew of Ken's inner struggle, the bad years preceding 1981, when both he and his team faltered. Nor did they know that he was so depressed after the opening game of that he actually considered quitting.

That isn't all people don't know about Ken Anderson. For instance, he was the Bengals third round draft choice in 1971 out of tiny Augustana College in Illinois. Augustana had a team described by many scouts as not being good enough to beat a top high school club. Yet Ken went from that atmosphere to an NFL starting position before the end of his rookie season. It's difficult to imagine the amount of hard work and dedication that was necessary for Ken to achieve so much so soon.

In addition, when Ken joined the Bengals he was following on the heels of two extremely popular quarterbacks. So when he took the job from them, the fans made him the villain, even though he won the position on ability and merit. The Bengals, at that time, were an expansion team playing in just their fourth season. The team was coached by Paul Brown, who was also one of its owners. Brown had seen glory years with the Cleveland Browns in the old All America Conference and then the NFL. He had a great reputation as a football genius. But he was also known for something else.

Brown was the man who first began calling plays for his quarterbacks, sending the plays in via messenger guards who shuttled in and out on each down. Though he had coached several great quarterbacks, notably Otto Graham, Brown always liked a low-key personality, a player content to carry out his game plan. Consequently, his quarterbacks often got the reputation of robots, players programmed to perform without having to think for themselves. Nothing could be further from the truth, yet that reputation also dogged Ken Anderson for years.

The fact that Ken is the consummate team player has also helped keep him out of the limelight as an individual. He has always felt that the team comes first, and that the greatness of a quarterback should be measured in how many titles his team has won. So fittingly, when the Bengals were down, Ken slipped even further out of sight. Yet despite all this he has always been happy in Cincinnati.

"I'd probably make more money playing in New York or Los Angeles," he once said. "But I wouldn't want to play in either place. I'm not saying I *wouldn't* play in either place, though. There is a difference."

The difference is that if Ken's team were located in a big city, that's where he'd be. He's also proved he isn't interested in squeezing every possible penny out of management by the fact that he has usually negotiated his own contracts and has never had a squabble with the ball club. He didn't feel the need for an agent or lawyer. In fact, he was an outstanding mathematics student at Augustana and continued his education in the off-season. In July of 1981, he got his law degree from Chase College of Law, part of Northern Kentucky University. So now Ken has a lawyer, one he can trust.

He is still one of the top quarterbacks in the National Football League, but also a guy who found that respect comes grudgingly, not necessarily from his peers, but from the Monday morning quarterbacks across the land. It's been quite a battle and it isn't over yet.

Ken Anderson was born on February 15, 1949, in Batavia, Illinois, a small town with a population of about 11,000. His father was a high school custodian and there have been stories written about how the son of a custodian grew up to be a pro quarterback. That tends to bother Ken.

"Too much is made of that," he once said. "My father is a tremendous man. He and I spent a great deal of time together when I was growing up. We always had a nice house and I had everything I wanted. I always enjoyed the times I spent with my family."

That seems very characteristic of Ken, who spends a great deal of time with his wife and two children today. At any rate, it wasn't long before he began playing sports as a youngster, though baseball and basketball were his early favorites. Football came later, and in his early years and nearly right through high school, he was a better baseball and basketball player than he was a football star.

Athletes who come out of small towns like Batavia often become local heroes, superstars whose reputations extend far beyond the town lines. There was a superstar in Batavia back then, but it wasn't Ken Anderson. It was Dan Issel, who lived right next door. Issel was a year ahead of Ken in school and was the town hero. He later became a basketball all-America at the University of Kentucky, and then a pro star, which he remains today. In fact, for a long time there were signs outside of town, which read:

"Welcome to Batavia, Home of Dan Issel."

So Ken began taking a back seat early, though in those days there were no real indications that he would be anything but a good all-around athlete.

When he reached Batavia High Ken was playing three sports, but baseball and basketball were still the primary ones. He wasn't even a quarterback then. His first two years he played mostly at defensive back. Ken continued growing during his high school years and by the time he was a senior he was just about at his present height of six foot three. During his junior year, he had also seen what big time recruiting could be like. Oh, no, it wasn't for him. He watched the parade of coaches and recruiters coming to see his next door neighbor, Dan Issel.

"Dan was the first real big timer to come out of Batavia," said Ken. "I guess nearly every major basketball school tried to get him and I can even remember Adolph Rupp himself coming right to the door."

Rupp, of course, was the long-time coach of Kentucky, a living legend, with the nickname of the Baron, and the whole scene must have made young Ken wonder if the same thing would be happening to him the next year.

Issel left for Kentucky in the fall of 1966. With Dan gone, maybe Ken would be the next one. But he just didn't have that kind of reputation, or the deeds to create it. In fact, Issel never remembered seeing Ken play quarterback at all in those years, and said that when the two used to play basketball together, he noticed how hard Ken used to have to work on everything.

"I honestly don't think anyone in Batavia thought Kenny would achieve what he has," Issel would say in later years.

By his senior year Kenny had made the changeover to quarterback, primarily to fill a gap created when the incumbent graduated. He always had a fine arm, stoked by his many years of throwing a baseball, and now he also had the size. One thing that there was never a question about was Ken's intelligence. He was an outstanding student all through school and applied that same kind of thinking to the athletic field.

So Kenny played all three sports once again as a senior and later admitted that he was slightly disappointed to realize that no big schools were interested. There would be no Adolph Rupps knocking on his door. In fact, they weren't even sending him letters. So he began working on getting academic and aid scholarships.

Finally, there were two local schools which showed an interest. North Park College in Chicago was one, and little Augustana in Rock Island, Illinois, was the other. He finally decided on Augustana, where he had a scholarship package which combined academics and also something for basketball and baseball. A school like Augustana cannot offer athletes the same kind of full boat that the big schools hand out.

Before he left for his first year, Ken also wrote a letter to the school asking if it would be all right if he tried out for the football team. The coach of the Vikings, Ralph Starenko answered that it was fine, adding, "We're always looking for defensive backs."

It's pretty incredible to think about a future NFL quarterback who didn't even have enough of a reputation as a quarterback in high school to make a school such as Augustana aware of his presence and ability. At any rate, Ken went out and very quickly became a quarterback. He played football and basketball as a freshman, but after seeing how much it took out of him, he begged out of baseball. It was important to him to maintain his grades, which he always did. Basketball stayed on his schedule through his junior year. He stopped playing as a senior for the same reason—his studies.

Despite being a very small school, Augustana had fielded a football team since 1893, but the schools that they played weren't exactly household names. Some of the other colleges on the Augustana schedule were Carthage, North Central, Wheaton, Elmhurst, Illinois Wesleyan, Millikin, Monmouth, North Park, and Western Illinois. There would be no USC, Ohio State, Alabama, or Notre Dame for Ken to test himself against, or for the pro scouts to judge his talents.

Yet he didn't complain and went about becoming the best quarterback for Augustana that he could. He saw considerable action as a freshman, and by his sophomore year of 1968, he was the starter. That's when Ken began rewriting the Augustana record book, setting a number of marks that still stand at the little college today.

In a game against North Park on November 2, Ken really got hot. Using his strong arm to pinpoint receivers, Ken threw for 410 yards and five touchdowns. He also ran for another 49 yards to establish a total offense mark for the game of 459 yards. He was hot as a pistol all year, and as a soph, probably had his best year statistically.

He completed 136 of 239 passes that season, good for 2,117 yards and 20 touchdowns. His passing percentage was 56.9 and his 211 yards rushing gave him 2,328 yards in total offense. Great stats, but how much can it mean compiling them for Augustana? Ken didn't know and probably didn't think about it much, except perhaps for the fact that he met his first pro football scout that season. He was an old timer who worked for the Green Bay Packers, and their meetings were so brief and informal that Ken didn't even know his name.

Yet the old scout was instrumental in Ken's immediate future when after his second year the entire Augustana coaching staff left. Ken's first reaction was to transfer to a larger school at this point and play against better competition. He mentioned it to the old scout who advised him to stay where he was and finish up. For whatever reason, Ken let the old man's advice guide him and decided not to transfer.

The Vikings had been 6–3 in 1968, and despite the coaching change which brought Ben Newcomb onto the scene, had another solid team in 1969. And by that time, there were some other people beginning to notice that Augustana College had a big quarterback with a strong arm, and a guy who seemed to really know what he was doing.

Though Ken didn't know it, there were now some things going on behind the scene that would greatly affect his future. Since his hometown of Batavia is located some forty miles from Chicago, Ken has always been a Chicago Bears fan. He remembers watching them when he was growing up and cheering guys like Billy Wade, Harlon Hill, Rudy Bukich, and Richie Petitbon, and wishing he could play for them some day. That was just a pipe dream then, but ironically, the Bears might have been the first pro team to hear about his play at Augustana.

It seems that long-time Chicago broadcaster Jack Brickhouse had a daughter attending Augustana. Every year she would beg her father to attend the Homecoming Game. In the fall of 1967 his schedule permitted it and Brickhouse went.

"I'm sitting in the stands watching the game and pretty soon I can't take my eyes off the Augustana quarterback," Brickhouse said. "My God, you never saw so much poise, and he wasn't exactly playing with the Four Horsemen and Seven Mules (a reference to the nickname of a great Notre Dame team of the past). It was Ken, of course, and he was just a freshman then. The next year when I saw him he was even better. So I told George Halas about him."

George Halas, of course, was the man who ran the Bears. Whatever the reason, Ken claims the Bears never scouted him in person and thus never considered drafting him. But by his junior year some other teams were beginning to take an interest. The club was on its way to a 7–2 year and Ken was once again playing fine football. His new coach, Ben Newcomb, began raving about his passing, and one of the opposing coaches whose team was beaten by Ken's arm, went as far as to call him "the best pro prospect I have seen."

All this talk reached the ears of Paul Brown, who was

owner and coach of the new NFL franchise in Cincinnati, the Bengals, which had just begun play in 1968. Naturally, Brown was on the lookout for good young players to develop, and it didn't matter if they were playing at Michigan State or Augustana. So hearing the raves, he sent his son, Pete, then the Bengals' personnel director, to Rock Island to see Ken play. The report on the kid playing for the tiny school surprised everyone.

"Great arm and a brilliant mind," it read, in part. "A first-round choice if he had gone to a big school. Still, a worthwhile first-day pick for us."

That in file, Coach Brown wanted to know more. So he next sent his quarterback coach, Bill Walsh, to Augustana. Walsh, who was well on his way to becoming a genius at developing quarterbacks, was very impressed, also. He wrote that Ken was "an excellent prospect, equal to, or better than Dennis Shaw, Mike Phipps, and Terry Hanratty," the top quarterbacks coming out of college around that time.

So the Bengals kept watching. In his senior year of 1970, the Vikings had lost many players to graduation and did not do very well, even within their own league. Ken also missed several games toward the end with injuries, but he still put together another fine season, and there was plenty of opportunity to see him throw the ball. In an October game against Carroll that year, he completed 25 of 58 passes. So it wasn't difficult for a scout to see him in action.

This time Paul Brown sent his other son, Mike, to watch Ken. Mike was the Bengals' Assistant General Manager, and he was the third person to bring the coach back a raving review, saying that Ken was "the best quarterback prospect I have seen in college," adding in his analysis that Ken was "more accurate than (Greg) Landry and (Roman) Gabriel were at this stage."

Yet the Bengals weren't the only team that knew about Ken then. Perhaps they did scout him more extensively than the others, but Gil Brandt of the Dallas

Cowboys, claimed a few years later that most of the clubs knew about Ken.

"Everybody knew about him in college," said Brandt, always one of the most astute judges of talent in the business. "We had Jack Mollenkopf, the old Purdue coach, working for us then and we sent him to see Anderson three times. The problem was that there were so many questions about the guy.

"For one thing, he got hurt the last two games and didn't finish the season. And besides that, he was playing in what we considered a high school league. I wasn't sure that Spring Branch High in Texas couldn't beat Augustana. So you become reluctant to draft a player in the high rounds from a school that small."

The 1970 season was a banner year for top flight senior college quarterbacks. There was Jim Plunkett at Stanford, Joe Theismann from Notre Dame, Archie Manning at Mississippi, all major stars and Heisman Trophy candidates. Then there was the highly-touted Dan Pastorini at Santa Clara, Lynn Dickey at Kansas State, Scott Hunter from Alabama, Rex Kern of Ohio State, and several others who would be picked by the pros. With so many available, there was even less likelihood that a guy at Augustana would be picked high.

Ironically, Gil Brandt admitted some four years later, in 1974, that he had judged all those college quarterbacks from 1970 quite accurately—except Kenny. By 1974 he had Ken rated right behind Plunkett, and if he looked at them again today, there's a good chance he might have Ken at the top of the list.

So Ken finished his senior season at Augustana. He would up his career with 424 completions in 827 attempts for a 51.3 percentage and 6,131 yards. He had thrown for 48 touchdowns and with his 548 yards rushing had a total offense of 6,679 yards. Augustana or not, it was quite a record. After that he settled in to study, wanting to maintain his 3.4 average in math, which he did.

When Ken first went to Augustana, he thought he wanted to be a teacher. Had he not been drafted, that's undoubtedly what he would have done. But by then he was well aware that he could very well be picked, even if it was on a late round. And he was pretty sure he wanted to give pro ball a try.

The Bengals, as mentioned, began play in 1968 and had a typical first-year expansion record of 3–11. The following season Paul Brown made Greg Cook, a quarterback out of Cincinnati, his first draft choice. He also picked some other solid players that year, like linebacker Bill Bergey and cornerback Ken Riley. The two leagues had not yet merged completely then, and the Bengals were in the old American League, the AFL. In 1969 they improved slightly to a 4–9–1 mark, but Greg Cook surprised everyone by maturing very quickly and actually leading the AFL in passing. It looked as if the Bengals had a quarterback they could depend on for ten or fifteen years.

But the next year fate took a hand. In 1970 the two leagues completed their merger and the Bengals were placed in the American Conference Central Division, which also had a couple of NFL teams represented, the Cleveland Browns and Pittsburgh Steelers, as well as the Houston Oilers. It was to become one of the most competitive divisions in the league.

At any rate, the Bengals again drafted well, getting a super defensive tackle in Mike Reid and another outstanding cornerback in Lemar Parrish, among others. The problem was Greg Cook. The already popular quarterback sustained a shoulder injury and was out of action indefinitely. That's when Virgil Carter came to the rescue.

Carter was a small, mobile quarterback with a questionable arm. But like Ken, he was a mathematics major and very intelligent. After sitting the bench with the Chicago Bears and letting management know how he felt about it, Carter came over to Cincinnati. Scramblers are sometimes effective with expansion teams weak in the offensive line, and Carter put together a heroic season. So did the rest of the Bengals. They surprised the football world by finishing 8–6 in just their third year and what's more, winning their division.

Along the way they had whipped the likes of the Oakland Raiders and the Browns, and then clinched the division with a whopping 45–7 victory over Boston. The largest crowd in Cincinnati sports history, some 60,157 fans, watched the game and made the Bengals the darlings of the town. A playoff loss to Baltimore barely dimmed their amazing achievement. Paul Brown was voted NFL Coach of the Year, and Virgil Carter was looked upon as a genuine folk hero.

Still, when it was time for the 1971 draft, Coach Brown and his staff were looking for another quarterback. Cook's shoulder was still a big question mark, and Carter, despite his 1970 heroics, had obvious shortcomings. Guys like Plunkett, Manning, and Pastorini went early, 1–2–3 in fact. Brown knew he couldn't get them, and had decided that the man he wanted was Ken Anderson. He gambled that other clubs would pass over Ken early because of his small-college background.

"When we got to the third round we decided we had stretched our luck far enough," Brown said. "We grabbed Kenny, and it turned out to be a good thing. We found out later that Atlanta, which picked before us on the next round, was all ready to take him."

So there it was. Ken Anderson from tiny Augustana college was the 67th college player picked in the entire country. It was even hard for him to fathom.

"I left Rock Island at seven in the morning the next day," Ken remembered. "I had known Paul Brown as a legend in Cleveland when I was growing up and before the end of the day I was sitting across from him in his office. He told me how surprised he was that I had still been available on the third round and how glad he was to have me. I just sat there. I couldn't believe it."

To sign a contract was no real problem. It's the top choices, the first-rounders, who usually go for the big bucks, complete with agents, lawyers, and all kinds of advisors. Third round choices don't have the same kind of leverage, unless they threaten to go to Canada, as Joe Theismann actually did. Still, many third-rounders and lower still have agents to negotiate for them. Ken wasn't about to do that. He began his custom of negotiating for himself and not revealing the contract publicly. Rumor had it that he signed for a "bargain basement price" as a rookie.

"Let's say I'm making more money than I would have as a teacher," was all he'd reveal. "I don't believe in giving details of contracts because that's the kind of thing I like to keep personal. Certainly I care how much money I make, but it's between me and the team."

In some ways, Ken Anderson was the right man in the wrong place in 1971. Cincinnati fans were in for several major disappointments during the year and they had to take it out on someone. For beginners, it was learned right at the outset that Greg Cook's damaged shoulder would keep him from playing, perhaps for the entire season. The fans had loved Cook when he came on the scene in 1969. Many saw him as a Joe Namath type, who cut a dashing figure with the ladies and had the same kind of charisma as the Jets Super Bowl hero. Plus he was a winner.

Virgil Carter caught their fancy because he was the underdog, a little guy who had been drummed out of Chicago and responded by leading the Bengals to a divisional title. The knowledgeable ones realized he wasn't a longterm solution, but there was a great deal of admiration and appreciation for the thrills he had given everyone in 1970. So they were rooting for him.

Then along came Ken Anderson—quiet, unassuming Ken Anderson. By rights, he should have fit right in to the Cincinnati lifestyle, always rather conservative. As Ken himself said a few years later:

"I don't really get involved in politics, but you could say I'm a conservative person. It just so happens that I coincide with Cincinnati. A different guy coming in here, well, maybe the mesh wouldn't work as well."

But in Ken's rookie year the mesh didn't really work, for the fans, resentful that Cook couldn't play, and seeing this rookie from the tiny college trying to take Carter's job, made him the villain. It didn't help matters, either, when the team reverted to its expansion ways.

As is often the case with an expansion team that finds success quickly, the talent and depth weren't really there. The good season, in the Bengals case 1970, was a combination of grit, the breaks, some opportunism, and outright luck. After the Bengals of 1971 won their open-er impressively, a 37–14 victory over Philadelphia, they promptly fell on their collective faces and lost seven straight ballgames. In five of those games they lost by a margin of four points or fewer. But they lost. And a 1–7 record isn't going to make anybody happy.

With the team losing, Ken began getting more of a chance to play. Carter, with his rollouts and short pass-ing game had a high completion percentage, so to the average fan he was doing well. Therefore, whenever he was replaced by Ken there was more than a smattering of boos among the fans at Riverfront Stadium.

Coach Brown and his staff brought Ken along slowly. Since they called the plays they kept the game con-servative. But they needn't have worried. It was obvious from the start that Ken kept mistakes to a minimum. Unlike many first and second year quarterbacks, he didn't throw a whole lot of interceptions, knowing when to eat the ball or throw it away. His intelligence on the gridiron could be seen immediately.

After losing their seventh straight, the club bounced back to defeat Denver, Houston, and San Diego. But just when it seemed they were getting on the right track they nosedived again and lost their last three, to finish the season at 4–10.

Ken got a couple of late season starts and pitched enough relief to put together a substantial rookie year. He completed 72 of 131 passes for 777 yards and a 55.0 completion percentage. He tossed five scoring passes and had just four intercepted. In addition, he also showed he could run with the ball, gaining 125 yards on 22 carries for a 5.2 average and another score.

The Bengals had a good draft in '72, tabbing defensive end Sherman White, safety Tommy Casanova, and linebacker Jim LeClair on the first three rounds. The club was still building. Once again there was disappointment involving Greg Cook. The budding star of 1969 couldn't seem to shake the shoulder miseries that were beginning to appear chronic. Whenever he'd try to really throw the problems would return.

That left it between Ken and Virgil Carter for the starting job. Once again Carter was the sentimental favorite among the fans who didn't hesitate to let their feelings known in the preseason games. But the handwriting was on the wall. Ken was bigger and stronger, and could throw better. And he was learning all the time.

"Every top quarterback has his attributes," he said. "I don't do things the way Fran Tarkenton does and I can't throw the ball as hard as Terry Bradshaw, though I can throw hard if necessary. But there are a lot of times when you can't throw the ball as hard as you'd like because it has to go over or around people. That was one of the hardest things I've had to work at, learning how to put 'touch' on the ball."

Those were the little things a quarterback can't get at a school like Augustana, but Ken was learning fast. There was even a story about this time of a reporter asking Coach Brown if anything about training camp excited him. Brown, in his usual manner, said something to the effect that things were going about as expected.

Later, when the reporter had retired to write his story, Brown is said to have sought the man out and said:

"You want to know what excites me. We've found ourselves a real man. He's our whole future and he's out there now throwing passes. Why don't you go out and see for yourself."

The coach, of course, was referring to Ken. And he proved it by naming Ken to open the 1972 season as the Bengals' starting quarterback. The decision didn't please the fans, most of whom still felt Carter should have the job. But in just one year Ken had won the starting role, and those who knew him well were pretty sure he wasn't going to lose it.

Ken was continuing to work very hard at learning his trade. He had already developed a routine that he followed all season long. Each weekday night he would review game films of the upcoming opponent for two hours. He also went over all the computerized scouting reports on the team, reports that gave the tendencies of the defense, and how they could be expected to react to certain offensive situations. By Wednesday the coaches had set up the game plan for Sunday and Ken would go over it a number of times with Bill Walsh, the quarterback coach. By Sunday he was ready.

The game plan usually took into consideration Ken's lack of experience and was fairly conservative, at least in 1972. The club would try to play a ball control game and hopefully not let things get out of hand early. A solid, 31–7, victory over New England in the opener was a good beginning. Ken played very well, showing poise and patience, executing the plays in an almost flawless fashion. In addition, the defense, helped by the top three draft choices, looked much improved over 1971.

Game two produced some real excitement, a 15–10 upset of rival Pittsburgh, and Bengal fans began thinking more about 1970 than 1971. They also began to feel that perhaps Coach Brown was right after all. Ken Anderson was the quarterback of the future.

The Bengals were not going to pull off any miracles in '72, but they did put together a solid season, duplicating their record of 1970 at 8–6. Only this time it wasn't good enough to get them into the playoffs. Yet they seemed to be finding themselves as a team, and surely they had found themselves a quarterback.

For the season Ken completed 171 of 301 passes for 1,918 yards and a 56.8 completion percentage. He had a very low number of intercepts with seven, but only threw seven TD passes. That statistic would have to be improved upon. Yet he was obviously a very accurate quarterback. His completion percentage his first two years was better than 55 percent, and that's unusual for a young and basically inexperienced quarterback. Perhaps Brown's messenger system had something to do with it.

"Because we send in the plays our quarterbacks are free to concentrate exclusively on execution and the progression of pass receivers," the coach said. "Mentally, that's just about a fulltime job. I'd rather have the quarterback concentrating on this instead of having to worry about strategy."

In 1973, the Bengals went out and got Ken something he had been lacking. They drafted wide receiver Isaac Curtis from San Diego State; a speedburner who would represent a real deep threat, a home run catcher, something the club had been lacking and perhaps one of the reasons Ken threw so few touchdown passes the past season. They also picked up a couple of running backs who would help, halfback Lenvil Elliott and fullback Boobie Clark.

Ken now had more tools to work with. Boobie Clark would give him a power back and would be named AFC Rookie of the Year for his efforts. Curtis would earn a starting berth and be outstanding, complimenting Chip Myers, the other wide receiver and more of a pattern runner; and the fine tight end, Bob Trumpy. It would be the year the Bengals became an outstanding team.

But it didn't start out that way as the team split its first eight games, beating Houston, San Diego, Pittsburgh and Kansas City, but losing to Denver, Cleveland, those same Steelers, and powerful Dallas. With a 4–4 mark it didn't look as if the club was going anywhere. But after eight games the new players were fully integrated into the systems and things really fell into place.

First Buffalo fell, 16–13; then the Jets, 20–14. St. Louis was victim number three, 42–24, followed by a win over Minnesota, 27–0. It was the first time the Vikes were shut out in 162 games. After that the Bengals whipped Cleveland, 34–17, and Houston in a dramatic finale, 27–24. Six straight victories gave the club a 10–4 record and their second AFC Central title in four years.

Along the way Ken had his finest year, completing 179 of 329 for 2,428 yards and 18 big touchdowns. His passing percentage was a solid 54.4 and he threw just 12 intercepts. The drafting of Isaac Curtis had been a big difference. The fleet receiver grabbed 45 passes as a rookie, averaging 18.7 yards a catch, and he was on the receiving end of nine of Ken's scoring aerials.

So the club went into the playoffs with high hopes. They would face the defending Super Bowl champs, the Miami Dolphins, a powerhouse team bent on repeating. So despite the fine year, the young Bengals were no match for the Bob Griese-Larry Csonka-Paul Warfield Dolphins, and Miami won easily, 34–16.

Even though the season ended on a downer, the Bengals still had to feel good about themselves. They had all the earmarks of a team with a bright future. And by all standards they seemed to have a quarterback with an equally bright future. Ken had unquestionably improved with each of his three seasons, yet he had still received little notice outside of Cincinnati and was unknown to the majority of pro football fa

The 1974 season turned out to be a strange one in several ways. First of all, the team once again followed an outstanding year with a mediocre one. With basically the same cast of characters the Bengals went from a division winning 10–4 record to the middle of the pack at 7–7. But while this was happening Ken Anderson finally emerged as one of the undeniably fine quarterbacks in all of football.

Ken was outstanding from the very first game, hitting his passes at a nearly 65 percent clip all season long. For the most part the offense was in good hands. It was the defense that seemed to fade as the club lost games by scores of 20–17, 30–27, 34–21, and 23–19. They were putting points on the board, only the other team was putting more on.

But there were high spots, like a 33–7 thrashing of Cleveland, a 28–17 defeat of Washington, and another win over the Browns, 34–24. Then there was the game with Pittsburgh in early October. Coming in, the Super Bowl-bound Steelers were heavy favorites, but Ken Anderson began picking apart their vaunted Steel Curtain defense from the opening kickoff.

"The Steelers strategy was to drop their linebackers deep and take away our wide receivers," Ken said. "So I concentrated on throwing to our backs and picking up four to six yards a crack."

Short passes or not, it was still the NFL and the Steelers in 1974 were the league's best. But they didn't or couldn't adjust and Ken kept killing them. When the game ended the Bengals had a 17–10 win, and Ken had set an NFL record by completing 20 of the 22 passes he threw. It was a mark that still stands today. Yet after the game when the reporters crowded around to ask him about the record, Ken said:

"I didn't think about the record at all. I was only

thinking about winning the game. We've got a tremendous offensive line protecting me. Why don't you go talk to them?"

When someone mentioned Ken's comments to Coach Brown he didn't act surprised at all.

"Ken Anderson is a most unselfish ballplayer," the coach said. "He cares only about the team and about winning, not about personal glory or his statistics."

But as is often the case in sports, people measure you by your stats, sometimes looking at them as much or even more than the won-lost ledger. And in 1974 Ken Anderson's stats were eye-opening.

He completed 213 of 328 passes for 2,667 yards and an incredible 64.9 completion percentage. He threw for 18 touchdowns and had just ten picked off. In addition, he ran the ball 43 times for another 314 yards, a 7.3 average per carry. Though he was the leading passer in the entire National Football League still, recognition didn't come overnight. He was passed over when it came time to select the AFC quarterbacks to participate in the pro bowl All-Star game after the season. But those who knew him well were quite aware of what he was doing.

"I knew Kenny had a strong arm when he came here," said veteran wide receiver Chip Myers, "but I never thought he'd catch on so fast. They say that it takes quarterbacks five to seven years to reach their potential. Kenny did it in four. I remember when he first joined the team. You wondered who would listen to a quiet guy like that. But you listen, all right. He's quiet, but you listen."

Old friend Dan Issel was another who marveled at the success achieved by his hometown pal.

"I honestly don't think anyone in Batavia thought Kenny would achieve what he has," Issel said. "To be truthful about it, I was shocked to see him drafted so early. But the first time I saw him play I think he was something like 11 for 15 in the first half against Cleveland and I couldn't get over it. Now I wonder if he isn't the best quarterback in football."

Quarterback coach Bill Walsh, who was about to leave the team, was also proud of the way Ken had matured. But he wasn't that surprised because he knew, perhaps more than anyone else, how hard Ken had worked to get there.

"Ken was a totally raw, green football player when he got here," Walsh said. "I don't think Augustana could have stood up to any of the Los Angeles city high school teams then. But the best thing Ken did was immediately move to Cincinnati and sign within a week of the draft.

"He wanted to learn so badly that we worked together by the hour. Because we had other competent quarterbacks on the roster we didn't have to throw him to the wolves right away. We worked him in and without the intense pressure of having to do it all by himself, he came along very quickly."

The club received one blow before the 1975 season started. All pro tackle Mike Reid announced his retirement after just five seasons to pursue a career in music. Reid had anchored the defense, but a rookie from Pittsburgh, Gary Burley, would do a good job in his place. Now if the club could avoid injuries they hoped to have a better season.

This time the team got off to a real strong start. They whipped Cleveland in the opener, 24–17, and went from there, beating New Orleans, Houston, New England, Oakland, and Atlanta. It was the Bengals' best start ever, six straight wins, and they were again looking like one of the best teams in the league.

As usual, the offense was in good hands. Ken was having another brilliant season, as was Isaac Curtis and the rest of the offensive crew. As guard Dave Lapham said, "Every guy here felt if we gave Ken that extra second of protection, he'd kill people. And he was."

Ken and the offensive team had been remarkably consistent. The barometer for success and failure of the team seemed to fall with the defense. When they faltered, the team lost, usually in a high scoring donnybrook. When they played well and held the opposition, Ken and his offense took care of the results.

It was defensive lapses that led to the team's first loss, a 30–24 defeat by mighty Pittsburgh. They rebounded to squeak past Denver, 17–16, now had to face a solid Buffalo team with their great running back, O.J. Simpson. The game would be played on Monday night, so a huge national TV audience would be watching. Ken would be on display before a large portion of the country.

"We went into the game at 7–1, but we still needed a win to remain in a tie with Pittsburgh," Ken recalled. "O.J. was having another fantastic year so we had to figure he'd get big yardage and they would get points. To counter that we decided on a simple game plan. We would come out throwing."

That's just how the game developed, Simpson's legs versus Anderson's arm, although Buffalo did try to cross up the Bengal defense by throwing on their first possession. It didn't work and after that they went mainly to the Juice.

The first time the Bengals got the ball they put together a long drive, Ken lumbering up his arm. They got the ball in close and Ken hit Lenvil Elliott from the five for the first score. The point was missed, but it was a 6–0 game. But Simpson quickly showed why he was the best running back in the game, going 59-yards to the Cincy 13. The Bills wound up with a field goal, cutting the Bengal lead to 6–3.

Early in the second period Ken went to work again. The big play on the drive was a 47-yard bomb to Curtis, putting the ball inside the 10. Halfback Stan Fritts ran for the score and the point made it 13–3. The Anderson-Simpson show continued for most of the second period. O.J. finally got a TD with about four minutes left, making it 13–10. But Ken went right back to work, drove his club downfield, then hit wide receiver Charlie Joiner from twenty yards out.

It was a 20–10 game at halftime. Ken was 16 for 23 for 198 yards and two scores, and the Juice had carried nine times for 154 yards. The game was developing into an incredible two-man duel.

Ken came out throwing in the third period, but Curtis fumbled the ball after a catch and the Bills ran it back to the 20. Several plays later O.J. scored again to narrow the margin to 20–17. The Monday night audience was really getting its money's worth. A Cincy field goal made it 23–17 at the end of three. It was still anybody's ballgame.

Early in the final session Ken had his team on the move again. He hit Joiner for a 33-yard gain and again for 14. From the Buffalo 11, Ken took off himself and ran it to the one. Stan Fritts then scored again and it was 30–17. Then midway through the final session, Buffalo's Joe Ferguson tossed a ten-yard TD pass to J.D. Hill, narrowing the margin to 30–24, and it looked as if the missed extra point might turn out to be crucial.

Ken wasn't content to sit on such a precarious lead. So he went back to the air, driving the Bengals downfield and setting up a short, 18-yard field goal that put the game on ice. The Bengals won it, 33–24, but that wasn't the whole story.

Simpson had been magnificent once again. The Juice carried 17 times for 197 yards, averaging better than ten yards a pop. But even with a performance like that he had to play second fiddle to Ken Anderson. Kenny had put the ball up 46 times, completing 30 of them for a whopping 447 yards and two scores. And with all that throwing he wasn't intercepted once. It wasn't possible to ignore the man now. He could play.

In typical fashion Ken passed his own performance off as "fun," preferring to talk about Simpson.

"I really enjoyed watching O.J. tonight," he said. "He's really something the way he moves, glides, darts, and finds the open spaces. He's much more entertaining in person than on television. Luckily we had a little more offense in the game than he did."

Notice how Ken referred to his offense as "we" and O.J.'s as "he." Again typical, always thinking of himself in terms of the team. But Simpson knew what he had seen that night, saying:

"I don't believe what I just saw Kenny Anderson do. He's just unbelievable."

When asked to comment on his quarterback's performance, Coach Brown also gave a low-key, analytical appraisal. But it was easy to see the amount of respect the coach had for his quarterback.

"Kenny's secret is that he's very bright," Coach Brown said. "He's no ordinary young man. He reminds me a lot of Otto Graham the way he knows how to pick his targets. When the primary receiver is covered he knows where to find a second or third choice."

Then the old coach gave his QB the ultimate compliment. "Otto is still number one in my book, but this young man is getting awfully close. I've never liked the self-centered athlete who knows that he's had fifty more blocks than his teammate, or that he's caught twenty more passes. Some guys keep track of every move they make, every yard, every tackle. A good football player thinks of the team as *his* team. That's Ken Anderson."

Though the Bengals were upset by Cleveland the following week, and were to lose again to mighty Pittsburgh, they won all the remaining games to finish at 11–3, their best mark ever. The Steelers won the division with a sensational, 12–2, mark. But the Bengals were in the playoffs once again, and that's what really mattered.

As for Ken, he had put together a second great season, again winning the NFL passing championship. This time he completed 228 of 377 passes for 3,169 yards and a 60.5 percentage. He threw for a career high 21 touchdowns and had just 11 picked off. He also ran for another 188 yards and two more scores. His favorite target was Isaac Curtis, who grabbed 44 for 934 yards, a 21.2 average and seven touchdowns. The two had become one of the most explosive passing combinations in the league.

Unfortunately, the Cincinnati season ended a week later. In a hard-fought ballgame, the Bengals were edged by the Oakland Raiders, 31–28. Ken and the offense did another fine job, but the defense couldn't handle the playoff-seasoned Raiders. The loss was a terrible disappointment for Ken and his teammates, and everyone else connected with the team. That was when Ken named Terry Bradshaw as the best quarterback in football. The Pittsburgh ace had led his club to a second consecutive Super Bowl triumph.

"It goes back to who won it all," Ken said.

But by now, Ken Anderson was also getting his due. He was finally named All-Pro and picked to represent the AFC in the Pro Bowl for the first time. He was also named the recipient of the Dodge-NFL player for his civic contributions as well as his athletic ability. In honor of Ken, a $10,000 Dodge scholarship fund was established in the Cincinnati area, and that made Ken very happy.

Ken had been active in much charity work around Cincinnati for some time. He had been honorary chairman of the Easter Seal drive in greater Cincinnati for two years and was also on the Board of Directors of Hope Cottage in Kentucky, an organization that houses and cares for orphans. In addition, Ken was a member of the Board of Directors of the Salvation Army in Cincinnati. So he certainly gave a good deal of his time to others, unlike many of today's athletes who are looking basically to get as much as they can out of their star status.

While Ken and his teammates had earned a great deal of respect with their showing in 1975, he had still not reached the status of a local hero. One reason was the town's other pro team, baseball's Cincinnati Reds. The Big Red Machine had won the World Series in 1975 and would win it again the following year. They were unquestionably the best team in baseball, and with the likes of Pete Rose, Johnny Bench, Joe Morgan, Dave Concepcion and others, there were more than enough heroes.

"Sure, everybody wants to be popular," Ken said, when asked about his low key image. "I wouldn't mind being a household name all over the country, but I'm not. And I won't allow it to worry me. I know I'm a good quarterback and I'm going to keep doing the best job I can. A lot of things go into being a superstar today. Take a guy like Joe Namath. He's a superstar because of his name, his charisma, the publicity he gets. I don't consider myself a superstar and playing in Cincinnati you don't get a lot of national publicity.

"I'm not knocking it and I'd be happy to spend my whole career here because we've got a good football team. I'm a home type, sure, and often when you say that people think you're a nothing personality. Certainly I'm not unhappy with my image, but I don't think I'm a nothing personality, either."

Then when someone asked Ken if he thought he was as good a quarterback as Namath, the pride and self-assurance that drives all the top ones came through.

"Overall, yes, I'm as good as Namath," he said.

When someone asked a similar question of Bill Walsh, who had tutored Ken in his early years, Walsh said that he felt Namath was the greatest quarterback in a given game that absolutely had to be won. Then he added, quickly:

"But at the moment I would say that Ken Anderson is the most effective quarterback over a fourteen-game season."

There was still the persistent criticism in some circles that as a Paul Brown quarterback, Ken was just a robot, a guy to run the plays without having to think on his own. This, of course, was nonsense. Bill Walsh, for one, said Ken was fully capable of calling his own plays, and Ken agreed, reminding everyone that he had the go-ahead to check off or call an audible at the line of scrimmage. Then, he defended the system.

"You know, in many ways the worst place to 'see' a game is on the field," he said. "The next worst is the sidelines. The guys in the spotter's booth have a view of the whole field and I'm happy to get all the help I can. Certainly, I'd like to be remembered as more than a mechanic. But that puts me in a tough spot. If I say I want to call the plays, then I'm bucking the system. If I say I'm satisfied to have them called for me, then I have no initiative as a quarterback.

"Let's put it this way, if it ever comes to me having to call the plays I think I'd do as well as anybody in the league."

It was almost like people wouldn't let Ken alone to be himself and perform within the context of his team. No matter what his achievement in the field, there was criticism at one level or another. It certainly would have gotten to someone who didn't have as even a disposition as Ken. His biggest worry was how to beat the next team the Bengals faced in the playoffs. Though the club certainly seemed strong enough to get there again in 1976, there were about to be some major changes.

The biggest one came in early January when Paul Brown decided to retire from coaching after forty-one years. He would remain as the team's general manager, vice president, and part owner, so he would still be very active in the operation. But the new coach would be his longtime aide, Bill Johnson.

In the draft that year the club picked up more offense. They took a speedy wide receiver from Oklahoma, Billy Brooks, then with a second first-round pick tabbed two-

time Heisman Trophy winner Archie Griffin of Ohio
State. Griffin was a small, chunky halfback who had
chewed up the yardage for Woody Hayes and the
Buckeyes, and Cincy people hoped he could do the same
thing in the pros to take some of the pressure off Ken.
The club also picked up kicker Chris Bahr and linebacker Reggie Williams. There was no reason to believe
that the Bengals wouldn't be right back in the hunt once
again.

What nobody knew at the time was that the Bengals
were slowly entering a period that would turn out to be
the roughest yet for both Ken and the ballclub. Before
the '76 season began, Ken said the club planned to run
more and try to achieve a better balance in the offense,
rather than "live and die by the pass." Then he added:

"My one goal is to win a world championship. If
you'll notice, the quarterbacks of the most successful
teams aren't rated as the top four or five passers. But
they win."

That last remark alluded to the fact that after the 1975
season Ken had the highest passing efficiency rating of
any quarterback ever. But to him that was purely a
statistical gimmick. He wanted to win that big one.

The club looked strong and confident under new
coach Johnson as the season got underway. They won
their opener over Denver before losing a 28–27 squeaker
to Baltimore. But then they reeled off three straight before being stopped by those Steelers again, 23–6. But
they rallied to win three more and going into game ten
with Houston the Bengals were 7–2 and two games ahead
of the Steelers, which had lost four games in the early
going and were now coming on. It turned out to be one
of the most exciting games of Ken's career.

Oiler quarterback Dan Pastorini, who came in the
same year as Ken, was out of action with an injury, and
veteran John Hadl was running the Houston attack.
Hadl came out smoking as if he was reliving his glory

days at San Diego and he quickly had the Oilers on top, 13–0. Meanwhile, Houston's defense was putting the clamps on Ken and company, and by halftime it was still a 13–3 ballgame.

Early in the third period Ken brought the Bengals into Houston territory at the 48. Then he calmly dropped back, spotted tight end Bob Trumpy down the middle and hit him perfectly with a toss that Trumpy converted into a 48-yard touchdown. The kick made it 13–10, but Hadl wasn't finished yet. He drove the Oilers in for another score making it 20–10. Ken, however, was now riding a hot streak and he brought the Bengals quickly downfield, then tossed a three yarder to Trumpy for another score. Now it was 20–17, Houston, as the third quarter ended.

The two defenses both tightened for most of the final session, but as the clock began winding down Ken got the Bengals moving on what was thought to be their final drive. With about four minutes left the ball was at the Houston one and Ken took it in himself for the go-ahead touchdown. The kick made it 24–20, giving Cincy the lead for the first time. All they had to do was hold the Oilers one more time.

But Hadl had it going that day and he wasn't about to be held. He moved the Oilers quickly and before anyone could look twice he was tossing a 13-yard TD pass to Ronnie Coleman. So it was 27–24 and the Bengals needed a field goal to tie. Ken was fighting the clock and had the ball at the Houston 43. But there were just three seconds left and he wasn't close enough. Ken himself takes up the story from there.

"I called a possession pass over the middle to Isaac Curtis. I was just thinking about getting a first down and hopefully giving our kicker, Chris Bahr, a crack at three points. When the Houston secondary rolled over to Isaac's side I looked back at Boobie Clark, who had come out of the backfield. But he was also covered. I was getting great protection back there so I had time to look back at Isaac again.

"He was open and I went to him. He caught the ball crossing the middle at full speed, broke a tackle, and went all the way for the score. It was really a spectacular ending, winning a big game like that with no time left."

So the Bengals were 9–2 with three games left and seemed a shoe-in for a playoff spot if not a divisional title. But in a head-to-head meeting with Pittsburgh the following week the Bengals couldn't pull it out. In a defensive struggle, the Steelers prevailed, 7–3. Then a week later, there was a 35–20 loss to Oakland. A season-ending win over the Jets put the club at 10–4. But they didn't take the divison and failed to qualify for the playoffs as a wild card. It was a terrible disappointment to the club and their new coach.

After his two fine years, Ken's stats were off slightly in '76. He completed 179 of 328 for 2,367 yards and a 53.0 percentage. He still managed nineteen TDs, but had a career high fourteen passes picked off. It was a good year, but compared to the past two seasons, the numbers weren't quite there. Yet the team had just missed at the end. No one could fault Ken, and indeed, no one tried to.

The 1977 season was mediocre in many ways and also marked a kind of transitional season for the ballclub. There suddenly seemed to be personnel changes at many positions. The continuity that seemed to be coming in 1974 and 1975, was now in question. Some of the veterans were being moved out, either in trades or through waivers, and players who had come on with a great deal of promise a year or two earlier, just weren't working out.

Archie Griffin, for instance, had never become the dominating runner he had been at Ohio State. He was a good pro back, but apparently not the kind who could control a ballgame, and definitely not a breakaway threat. Fullback Boobie Clark was Rookie of the Year in 1973, but by 1977 the club was drafting another fullback, Pete Johnson of Ohio State. There were the same kind of unsettled situations at a number of other positions.

So the team went 8–6 in 1977, a kind of win one, lose one, win one season. They were never in contention, never considered a threat. The team seemed to be on the downslide and as is often the case, the most visible player gets too much of the blame. Ken had perhaps his poorest season to date and the Cincinnati fans once again let him know it.

He completed 166 of 323 for 2,145 yards. His completion percentage was a career low 51.4, and he tossed just 11 scoring passes to go with 11 interceptions. Ken was just 28 years old at the end of the 1977 season, so by all right he should be clearly in his prime. The general mediocre play of the team undoubtedly affected him, too. He was hoping that the club would bounce back in '78, as it had done several times over the past few years.

It was hard to make a judgement on the club during the preseason when they split four games. But in the second half of that final preseason game with the Packers, Ken hurt his throwing hand. He did it on a charging lineman's helmet and X-rays showed a broken bone. Ken was on the sidelines when the season began. But after a couple of losses he came back.

The feeling was that Ken rushed back too soon because with the team going bad he felt he had to play, that Coach Johnson's job was in jeopardy. Though he didn't complain, those around him said the hand bothered him all year. On top of that, the club kept losing, to an embarrassing degree.

After five straight the club made a change, replacing Bill Johnson with Homer Rice. But in the first three weeks of Rice's tenure the club scored all of three points, being shut out twice. So a team that had been 11–3,

10–4, and 8–6 over the past three years was now the league doormat at 0–8.

Finally, there was a victory, 28–13, over Houston. But that didn't turn it around. Four more defeats followed and the Bengals were a humiliating 1–12. They managed to win their final three games to finish at 4–12, but oh how the mighty had fallen.

Ken was 173 of 319 for 2,219 yards and a 54.2 percentage. But the key to his season could be found in his ten touchdown passes as compared to twenty-two interceptions. You get that when you've got to constantly play from behind. As usual, Ken made no excuses. He still had that burning desire to play with a winner and hoped the club could rebuild and regroup. But he must have wondered just how the Bengal management felt when he saw the 1979 draft.

At the top of the Cincinnati list was a quarterback, and a good one. He was Jack Thompson, an all-American from Washington State, who had set an NCAA record by passing for 7,818 yards in three seasons. Born in American Samoa, Thompson had a nickname, the Throwin' Samoan, which fans could latch onto quite easily. The club had drafted other quarterbacks since Ken had arrived, but they were always lesser known players picked on low rounds with the obvious intention of looking at them as possible backups. But by making Jack Thompson their first choice, it seemed that the club was serving some kind of notice on Kenny.

There were a couple of additional picks that were interesting, as well. The second choice was Charles Alexander, a running back out of LSU. Apparently, the club had given up on Archie Griffin becoming a big runner. The third pick was a tight end, Dan Ross of Northeastern, whose job it would be to replace the retired Bob Trumpy.

Ken was still the starting quarterback when the 1979 season began, and for the first time since he joined the team he might well have wished he had become a schoolteacher after all. The club started the same way it had the season before—losing. They were shut out by Denver in the opener, then the defense gave up 51 points to Buffalo in the second game. The next two losses were by less than a touchdown, and then there was a blowout by Dallas. The club was finding new ways to lose each week. After losing their sixth straight, this one to Kansas City, they pulled a minor miracle by winning their first of the year against, of all teams, powerful Pittsburgh. But the handwriting was on the wall. The club was headed to a second straight, 4–12, season.

It was a physically demanding season for Ken. The offensive line was inexperienced and often porous. They allowed sixty sacks during the campaign, and subsequently Ken took a real beating. He managed to complete 55.7 percent of his passes, gaining 2,340 yards. And he threw sixteen TDs to just ten intercepts. In addition, he often had to run for his life and gained 235 yards on 28 carries for a career best, 8.4 yards a pop.

All in all, he had put in a good season under very adverse conditions. Yet throughout the year there were people constantly calling for a change to Jack Thompson, who had played enough to throw 87 passes and showed he had the potential to be a fine quarterback and a leader. For those front runners, the Ken Anderson era was over. It was time for a change.

Fortunately, the fans don't make those decisions. The only era that was over was that of Homer Rice. He had just been in the wrong place at the wrong time. Paul Brown, acting in his capacity as general manager, knew a change had to be made. He also knew it was time to get tough, and he wanted his new coach to reflect that. So he went out and got Forrest Gregg, a Hall of Famer who played tackle under Vince Lombardi at Green Bay when the Packers were winning title after title. Gregg was so respected by the tough Packer coach that in his book, *Run To Daylight,* Lombardi called Gregg "the finest player I ever coached."

Gregg had coached the Cleveland Browns from 1975 to 1977. Then in 1979 he moved up to Canada and coached the Toronto Argonauts of the CFL. The following year he was back in Cincinnati. Gregg had a tough, no-nonsense approach to coaching, much like his mentor Vince Lombardi. He took stock of the Bengal situation and was determined to change things immediately.

"For a couple of years things were very lax around here," admitted Ken, shortly after Gregg took over. "I don't think guys were in very good condition, but all that changed on day one when Forrest Gregg came in."

Veteran guard Dave Lapham agreed. "Before Coach Gregg came it was getting to the point where practice was a joke," he said. "There was a lot of fooling around and not much concentration in the meetings. All that was then reflected in our performance on Sundays."

"When you're not in condition you can't expect to play up to your abilities," Ken added. "Some did, but all forty-five players weren't going in that direction."

Defensive end Eddie Edwards mentioned another immediate result of the coaching change. "Before Coach Gregg if you weren't doing the job there was no one to tell you about it up front. No one was chewed out for being lousy. That changed fast."

Gregg began an immediate conditioning program and training camp in 1980 must have seemed more like a marine boot camp. He worked his players very hard. If the Bengals were goint to lose, it wouldn't be because the other team was in better shape. Gregg just wouldn't permit that to happen.

He also moved to stabilize the team's personnel. The top draft choice that year was a mammoth offensive tackle, all-American Anthony Munoz from USC. He would help immediately. But Coach Gregg was distressed by the kind of revolving door movement that had characterized the Bengals the last three years or so. It seemed like each season brought about a dozen new players to the team, either through the draft, trades, or the free agent lists. That caused a loss of cohesiveness that had characterized the team in 1974 and 1975. As one reporter characterized it:

"The Bengals had gone overboard on the youth movement and it was getting to the point where you wondered if the names on the back of the jerseys were for the players or the fans."

Even Ken commented on the many player moves. "There was a feeling that once you became a six-year veteran you wouldn't be around much longer," he said.

But all that was about to change. And as the Bengals prepared for the 1980 season the talk began shifting again to the quarterback question. Many fans were clamoring for a change to Jack Thompson. Ken was going into his tenth season and many felt he just couldn't cut it anymore. Plus the Throwin' Samoan had a kind of flare and verve about him that Ken lacked outwardly. At 6-3, 217 lbs., he was big and strong, and obviously a fine prospect.

What the fans were quick to forget was the outstanding seasons Ken had put together. The collapse of the team could no more be blamed on him than on a palm tree in Florida. But you know fans. Yesterday's hero is just that. With them it's what have you done for me lately.

Ken was having a good preseason. But in the final game he got another bad break. This time it was a knee injury, and while it didn't need surgery, he'd have to wear a brace and it would bother him all year. He also sprained an ankle and injured a breastbone during the course of the campaign. So one way or another, the fans would get to see a lot of Jack Thompson during the year.

In fact, the injury kept Ken out of the opener and the Bengals bowed to the Tampa Bay Buccaneers. Thompson showed his inexperience by completing just six of 21 for 47 yards. Ken started the second game against Miami and had completed just two of eight passes when he reinjured his leg. Thompson came in and this time played very well, completing 15 of 24 for 136 yards. He also helped the Bengals to a 14–10 lead before the Dolphins came back in the final period to win, 17–16.

So it was beginning to look like a year of musical quarterbacks. Ken's injuries would give Thompson a real shot to take the job. It had happened that way in football before, and Ken had to be wondering if his days in Cincinnati were numbered.

The next week it was the same thing. Ken started against Pittsburgh and looked sharp, completing eight of 10 for 63 yards, but again he reinjured the knee. Then Thompson came on and was a real hero, bringing the club from behind with 17 fourth-quarter points, including two touchdown tosses, as the Bengals won, 30–28, in an upset. Thompson was 9 of 18 for 122, and the Cincy fans were really beginning to take him to heart.

A loss to Houston followed, 13–10, with Ken sitting out. Then came another defeat, 14–9, to Green Bay. The club needed more offense and a week later against the Steelers again, Gregg turned back to Ken. This time the veteran responded with his best game of the year hitting on 17 of 32 for 179 yards and leading the team to a 17–16 upset.

The defense continued to improve, and so did Ken. He went all the way in a 14–0 defeat of Minnesota, completing 21 of 28 for 270 yards and a 55-yard TD toss. That was vintage Anderson, so maybe he was back to stay. The following week against Houston he seemed to have good stats, with 23 of 33 for 185 yards. But two intercepts and four sacks, plus 202 yards gained by Houston's Earl Campbell stuffed the Bengals, 23–3. The club was 3–5, improved over the season before, but still not a playoff threat.

A week later Ken and Thompson shared duties, but the San Diego Charger air express was too much for the Bengals and they lost, 31–14. Oakland whipped Cincinnati the next week, 28–17. The same pattern prevailed. Ken started, then his injuries flared up and Thompson came in. The youngster threw three intercepts to hurt his club's chances, but some wondered if Coach Gregg wasn't orchestrating a gradual changeover to Thompson. Meanwhile, the club was now 3–7 and virtually out of playoff contention.

They were to split their remaining six games to finish at 6–10, losing to Buffalo and Cleveland twice, and beating Kansas City, Baltimore, and Chicago. The quarterback situation stayed about the same, the two players splitting time about evenly, and Ken battling his injuries all year long.

"I can't remember one game during the year when Ken was 100 percent," said Coach Gregg. "He had something bothering him every week."

For the year, Ken completed 166 of 275 passes for 1,778 yards, lowest totals since his rookie year. His percentage was a solid 60.4, but he threw just six touchdowns as compared to 13 intercepts. Thompson, by way of comparison, completed 115 of 234 for 1,324 yards and just a 49.1 percentage. But he had 11 touchdown passes and 12 intercepts. Neither had a great year, but once again Cincy fans rooted for the youngster. Ken had to wonder if he'd ever be a favorite with his hometown fans.

After the season, there were stories about Ken's injuries, some of them related to his age, some even saying he was now injury prone, another bad rap.

"I went the first seven years of my career without an injury," Ken answered. "Anybody who plays ten years is going to have some injuries. If I had retired after seven or eight years they'd have said I was a durable quarterback who never got hurt."

Then in discussing the hit that caused his knee injury, Ken said, "You can go through ten years with no hits like that. I had three of them in one year."

His longtime friend and blocker, Dave Lapham, also defended Ken against the same claims.

"Some of the shots Ken took the last couple of years would have hurt anybody," he said. "One of the raps I've seen lately is that he won't play hurt. Let me tell you, his history has been just the opposite. He's played hurt plenty, and played well."

Of course, the big question now was whether Ken would withstand the challenge from Thompson in 1981. Coach Gregg had expected a rebuilding year, but now he wanted to win. The draft produced two explosive wide receivers, David Verser and Cris Collinsworth, as well as some other good players. Pete Johnson was becoming a force at fullback, and Anthony Munoz was already on the brink of becoming perhaps the most dominating offensive lineman in the league. The defense had solidified in 1980 and would hopefully be even better in '81. So Gregg felt the potential for a big season was right there already. And he planned to drive his players hard enough to get it.

Ken, too, knew this was a pivotal year. He was at that point in his career where he could easily be forced to the bench, or traded. If the word got out that he was washed up it could be several years before he got another real chance . . . if at all. Yet with all this on his mind, Ken still managed to go to school in the off-season, something he had been doing for a number of years. And in July he received his law degree from Chase College of Law. So he was planning for the future, but felt he had a lot of football left in him.

He came to camp in good shape and completely recovered from the various injuries of the year before. He was hoping to stay healthy during the season this time. Though he was playing well during camp and into the preseason, he could sense that the fans wanted Jack Thompson to start. In fact, as soon as Kenny made a mistake they let him know it.

"Nobody likes to be booed," he told a reporter. "I'm no different. Sure, I'd like to be popular. You hear it (the boos) and it hurts you. But you've got to try to block it out of your mind and most of the time I do a pretty good job of it.

"The thing that's tough is that I had a lot of success earlier in my career and for awhile was a pretty popular guy. Then we have a few losing seasons and our number one draft choice is a quarterback with a big reputation, and the tables start to turn. It gets to be kind of frustrating.

"I think all quarterbacks learn early that they're going to have their ups and downs with the fans. But I wonder how many of them know that Ken Anderson's worst critic is Ken Anderson. When I'm playing poorly, I'm harder on myself than they ever could be."

Unlike many other star players, Ken also lived in the town in which he played, and believed that he owed something back to the community, which he paid by his community service and his charity work.

"It is my community, too and I want to be involved," he told a TV interviewer. "We make this our home in the offseason and no matter what happens with football we're going to live in the Cincinnati area permanently."

No matter how you looked at it, Ken Anderson was not an easy guy to boo off the field. He just didn't deserve that kind of treatment. Indeed, the Bengal brass were talking as though Ken would be the starting quarterback once again, telling the media and anyone else that a healthy Anderson meant a great deal to the Bengal season, and they were hoping he would avoid the kinds of injuries that allowed him to complete just two of twelve starts in 1980.

So Ken seemed to be getting a solid vote of confidence

with the regular season just a few weeks away. But suddenly, without warning and with no apparent explanation, he began playing poorly. Very poorly. He was floundering around like a raw rookie, executing poorly, missing his receivers, and seemingly losing confidence rapidly. It was an old fashioned slump, perhaps brought on by Ken putting too much pressure on himself.

At the same time, Jack Thompson was still showing his talent for making the big plays, though he still lacked consistency. Ken, however, was finally named the starting quarterback for the opener against Seattle. He might have been helped by the fact that Thompson had an ankle sprain that cut his mobility. At any rate, some 41,000 fans turned out at Riverfront Stadium to see the Bengals open another season.

The club had a flashier look in 1981. They were wearing new uniforms with Bengal tiger stripes on the shoulders, and the helmet was now striped as well. Whether this would give them more bite only time would tell.

It was obvious from the first series of downs that Ken was shaky. He was tentative and overly careful, and that kind of play usually leads to mistakes. The first was a biggie, a Seattle interception that was run back 29 yards for a score. The Seahawks had the early lead, 7–0. Ken still couldn't shake the jitters. He was missing targets, and then threw a second intercept.

Seattle, meanwhile, was moving. They drove down deep and Jim Zorn hit Steve Largent with a 36-yard scoring pass. A one-yard TD run by Jim Jodat late in the period made it 21–0 after one. Ken was five for 15 for just 39 yards and the two intercepts, and the fans were booing him unmercilessly. Seeing how shaky Ken looked, Forrest Gregg made a decision. When the second quarter started the Bengal quarterback was Turk Schonert.

Turk Schonert? Who's he? With Thompson's ankle hurting, Schonert was the back-up, a third-stringer in his second year out of Stanford. And here he was, replacing Ken Anderson after one quarter of the first game. The ironic thing was that Schonert did the job. He was nine of 18 for 130 yards, and he actually helped the Bengals pull it out. They scored ten points in the second and third periods, and seven more in the fourth to win the game, 27–21. That had to make Ken's position more precarious. It was a turning point already.

"I put a lot of undue pressure on myself," Ken said. "There had been a great deal of controversy over who should play quarterback, and I thought if I was going to do anything, I'd have to be perfect. But no one can go out with that attitude and play perfectly. I was very tentative. You can't be that way. You've got to let it fly and not worry about it. Obviously, I played very badly. I had really hit bottom."

When Ken met with Coach Gregg after the game, the coach indicated that he would start Schonert the following week against the New York Jets, unless Thompson was ready. Then it would be the Throwin' Samoan. Where did that leave Ken, third string?

The game against the Jets would be at Shea Stadium in New York. Had it been at Riverfront, Ken didn't know if he could play, if he could face the hostile crowds again.

"Ken said if that game had not been on the road it would have broken him," his wife, Bonnie, said. "He never would have been able to play again."

So Ken was actually thinking about quitting, retiring right then and there before things could get worse. It's doubtful that he could have taken a demotion to third string. Then came one of those fateful decisions that really alters the course of history, or in this case, Cincinnati Bengal history. Sometimes during the next week Coach Gregg had a meeting with Kenny and soon afterward, the coach announced that Ken Anderson would get the starting shot against the Jets.

"My decision had a lot to do with Ken Anderson," the coach said. "What we talked about was personal, but I'll say this. Ken gave me the right answers, and with conviction."

So Ken began working with the first string again and said the decision and his play the week before helped restore his confidence.

"I was pretty loose," he said. "I figured things couldn't get any worse. I'd already hit rock bottom, so I stopped worrying. I was just going to go out there and do it."

When the Bengals got the ball for the first time the coaches immediately sent a pass play into the huddle. Ken got the word and then said to his teammates: "This is a pass, get ready to cover," meaning the ball would probably be intercepted. But his wisecrack kind of broke the tension, and after that everybody went out and played ball.

But it was the Jets who took charge at the beginning, building a 17–3 lead. Still, Ken was in there pitching. He led the club on a drive from about midfield and hit wide receiver Steve Kreider from the seven for a score, making it 17–10 at the half.

After the Jets started the third period with a field goal, Ken went to work again. He drove the Bengals 56 yards with Archie Griffin scoring from the one. That made it 20–17 after three. Then in the fourth period another Jets field goal upped it to 23–17. But Ken took the Bengals on another long march, this one of 67 yards ending with a three-yard TD toss to Griffin. The Bengals now led 24–23. A Jets fumble led to another Cincy score and a late Jet touchdown only brought it to 31–30. The Bengals had another come-from-behind win.

As for Ken, he looked like his old self, connecting on 21 of 33 passes for 246 yards and a pair of TD's. He had an outstanding receiving corps now. The veteran Curtis was still dangerous, having caught five passes for 108 yards against the Jets. Dan Ross was becoming one of the best tight ends in the league, and rookie Cris Collinsworth looked like a rare find and had become the other starter. Steve Kreider and gamebreaker David Verser were outstanding backups. If Ken found his old consistency, watch out.

There was a brief setback the next week as Cincy lost to Cleveland, 20–17. Once again they tried to come from behind after trailing 13–0 at the half, but this time they fell short. Still, Ken had a fine game, completing 16 of 25 for 238 yards and a 41-yard TD toss to Collinsborth. The quarterback job was once again his if he could stay healthy.

Then, the following week, the club seemed to put it all together. They won a hard-fought, 27–24, victory over a very good Buffalo team, with Ken hitting 28 of 40 for 328 yards and three scores. He led the club on scoring drives of 97, 91, 84, 70, and 58 yards. It was a beautiful effort.

"I don't know how anyone can play a better football game than Kenny did," said Coach Gregg.

Ken was now the third best passer in the AFC and moving up. He hit 30 of 52 for 290 yards against Houston, but the club lost, 17–10. They would have to get more running to balance things out. The club was 3–2, tied with Houston and Pittsburgh for the division lead, with the Browns a game behind. It was still a wide-open race, but win one, lose one wasn't the way to do it. The team would have to make a move.

They got off to a good start against the Colts, winning easily, 41–19, as Ken once again led with way. This time he completed 21 of 27 passes for 257 yards and three scores. Tight end Ross caught seven passes for 106 yards.

"Dan isn't as big or fast as some of the other tight ends in the league," Ken said, "but I'd rather him in there than anyone else."

Ken also acknowledged that aside from that opening game he was off to the best start of his career, adding: "But there's a long way to go, for me and for us."

Then the following week the Bengals went a long way toward showing everyone they were for real. They whipped the Steelers soundly, 34–7, with Ken hitting 16 of 28 for a whopping 346 yards and two more scores, including a 73-yard TD bomb to David Verser. Plus the Bengal defense shut the door on Terry Bradshaw and company. The Bengals were now atop the AFC Central at 5–2, and Ken was the third leading passer in the NFL behind Craig Morton of Denver and Dan Fouts of San Diego. He was doing the job.

"We've got that old feeling back again," said guard Dave Lapham. "We know if we give Ken that extra second of protection he'll kill people, just like he did back in '74 and '75."

There was a setback the following week, a 17–7 upset by the New Orleans Saints. Ken was 13 of 21 for 117 yards when he was knocked unconscious by defensive end Elois Grooms in the third period. A rusty Jack Thompson had to finish up and was just six for 20 as he tried to bring the club from behind.

Fortunately, Ken wasn't hurt badly and was back at the helm the next week, leading the Bengals past the Oilers, 34–21, as he hit on 21 of 30 for 281 yards and three scores. The club was at 6–3, a game ahead of Pittsburgh. Pete Johnson had a big game with 114 yards and was the sixth leading runner in the AFC. Both Collinsworth and Ross had 38 catches after nine games, and Ken had thrown 15 TD passes while being intercepted just four times. He was completing 63.2 percent of his passes and trailed only Morton in the NFL passing race. The Bengal offense seemed in high gear.

A 40–17 win over the Chargers followed. It was significant because the game was in San Diego and the Chargers have one of the most explosive offenses in the league. Yet the Bengal defense held Dan Fouts and Company, while Ken hit on 18 of 28 for 288 yards and two scores. Plus he did that in less than three quarters since he had to leave the game with a shoulder injury. Now Cincy fans kept their fingers crossed. No one was calling for a quarterback change, and they didn't want to be forced into one.

"The shoulder is very sore," Ken said, afterwards. "I don't even know how it happened. The first time I was hit in the back and it just knocked the wind out of me a little."

It was Ken's left shoulder that was hurt, but he was back in the following week against the Rams. He must have been hurting, because he only had a nine for 21 games, for 76 yards. But the defense did the job. Thompson finished up in relief and the Bengals won again, 24–10. The club was 8–3 with a two-game lead over Pittsburgh and three over Houston and Cleveland. There were very few doubters left. The Bengals were for real.

"It's been a fun year," Ken said, despite the sore shoulder. "Everybody is playing well, and like I've said 100 times before, a quarterback plays as well as the people around him."

Still a team man first. Ken then went out and put together another brilliant afternoon. He was 25 of 37 against the Broncos, good for 396 yards and two scores as the Bengals won, 38–21. Tight end Ross had seven catches for 123 yards and Pete Johnson bulled for 99. And there was now little doubt that Ken Anderson was having his best year ever. And against Denver the club set a Cincy record with 571 yards total offense.

Next the Browns fell, 41–21, with Ken 26 of 32 for 235 yards and three scores. That performance enabled him to take over the NFL passing lead with an incredible 104.2 efficiency rating. Then the next week the Bengal express was derailed. The other surprise team in the league, the San Francisco 49ers, did it with a 21–3 victory. Again Ken was hurt in the third period, suffering a sprained toe and leaving the game after completing 11 of 20 with two intercepts. It wasn't a good day.

But this team didn't quit. A week later they won a big game, 17–10 over the Steelers, as Ken was 21 of 35 for 215 yards. The victory gave the Bengals the AFC Central title. Like the rest of his teammates, Kenny was elated.

"I can't describe the feeling that winning it in Pittsburgh gives me," he said, still nursing the painful toe. "They have been rivals of ours for a long time."

A week later the regular season ended with a 30–28 victory over Atlanta, with Ken throwing 18 of 34 for 299 yards. The team finished with a 12–4 mark and now had to get ready for the playoffs. But what a year it had been for Ken and his teammates.

The veteran quarterback was the NFL passing champion for a third time, and once again an all-Pro. He finished with 300 completions in 479 tries, career highs, good for a percentage of 62.6 and another high of 3,754 yards. His 29 touchdown passes were also a career best, and he threw just 10 intercepts. He was also the club's second best runner with 300 yards on 46 carries for a 6.5 average, best on the team.

Fullback Johnson had his first 1,000-yard season, getting 1,077, while tight end Ross had 71 catches for 910 yards, third best in the AFC. Rookie Collinsworth had 67 catches for 1,009 yards and eight TDs. Isaac Curtis and Steve Kreider both had 37 catches, while Johnson had 46 coming out of the backfield. Ken had really spread the goodies around. Now the club had to get ready for its first playoff game against Buffalo, which had beaten the Jets in the wild card contest.

It was a confident Bengal team going into the playoffs. Though it was their first post-season appearance since 1975, under the motivational influence of Coach Gregg they felt they could go all the way, and they came out strong against the Bills.

A 27-yard punt return by Mike Fuller set up the first Cincy drive, Ken taking them 42 yards with Charles Alexander scoring from the four. Jim Breech's kick made it 7–0. A Ken Riley interception set up the second drive, a 48-yard march with Johnson plunging over from the one. After a quarter it was a 14–0 game.

Buffalo got one back in the second period, Joe Cribbs scoring from the one, they then tied it early in the third when the elusive Cribbs ran 44-yards for a score. Then late in the period Alexander scored on a 20-yard scamper, only to have the Bills come back early in the fourth on a Joe Ferguson pass to Jerry Butler. So it was 21–21, and still anyone's game, with time starting to run down.

Then midway through the period the Bengals got the ball and Kenny took over. He started the club moving. The big play was a 42-yard pass to Steve Kreider. Several plays later Kenny hit Collinsworth from 16-yards out for the score. That made it 28–21, and that's the way it ended. The Bengals were now in the AFC title game, and would host the San Diego Chargers.

After the game, Coach Gregg gave credit where it was certainly due.

"I want to say up front that I appreciate Paul Brown giving me a chance to coach this team," he said. "But a lot of the reason we are here today is standing right over there."

The coach then pointed to Ken Anderson, and rookie Cris Collinsworth was quick to echo the praise.

"Ken means so much to us in the huddle," said Collinsworth. "He's not a cheerleader out there. It's almost like he gets bored. But he keeps us all calm and under control. I get more nervous watching games on TV than I do out on the field with Kenny."

Ken had completed 14 of 21 passes for 192 yards against the Bills. He didn't throw that much, just when he had to. And he made those count. Against San Diego and their air-minded attack, he might have to throw a lot more. And before the San Diego game, Ken learned he had been named recipient of *The Sporting News* Marboro Award as 1981 NFL Player of the Year. So the recognition was coming. And once again Ken tended to spread it around.

"It's tough to give individual awards in a team sport," he said. "Those awards come because everybody has been playing well. There's no doubt I've been playing well, but so have my teammates. When you get awards like this, part of it has to go to everybody. And the real satisfaction is winning again. This just adds a special flair to it all."

The day of the AFC title game there was another opponent that both clubs would have to face—the weather. Riverfront Stadium was in the deep freeze. Temperatures plunged to nine below zero and the winds were gusting to 35 miles per hour. The wind-chill factor was a dangerous 59 degrees below zero. There was even some thought of calling the game off.

If the awful weather favored anyone it would be the Bengals, used to playing in the midwestern winters. The Chargers were used to sunny, balmy San Diego weather. But this was a football game and there could be no excuses, especially when two of the best passing quarterbacks in football were matched up.

The Bengals drew first blood when Jim Breach kicked a 31-yard field goal in the first period. Later in the session Ken marched the club downfield and hit backup tight end M.L. Harris on an eight-yard scoring pass. That made it 10–0.

But the Chargers drew close in the second period when Fouts hit his all-Pro tight end Kellen Winslow on a screen pass which he ran in for a 33-yard touchdown. Then in the second half it was all Bengals. Ken hit the key passes while Fouts missed. Breech kicked a third period field goal and in the final period Ken hit Don

Bass for a three-yard score. The final was a convincing 27–7. The Bengals had done it. They were AFC champs and headed for the Super Bowl.

After the game, someone asked Kenny how cold it was on the field.

"It wasn't really that bad," he answered. "I've been colder at other times."

Maybe all those times he had been booed in the past. In fact, he was the only player to suffer from frostbite, getting a touch of it on his right ear. But it wasn't serious. More important were his 14 of 22 passes for 161 yards. He also ran five times for another 39 yards which kept the Charger defense honest. It was quite a performance under the circumstances.

Now the Bengals would be going to the big one and it would be an interesting matchup. The San Francisco 49ers, like the Bengals, were just 6–10 in 1980, and had turned things all the way around to 13–3. Like Cincy, they were for real, in fact they had beaten the Bengals soundly, 21–3, in the regular season. Their quarterback was a youngster out of Notre Dame, Joe Montana, who was in his first season of real stardom. In addition, there was a common denominator linking Ken to Montana.

The 49ers coach was Bill Walsh, the man Ken said had "made me" when he was an assistant at Cincinnati in Ken's early years. Walsh was now recognized as an offensive genius, especially when it came to developing quarterbacks and passing attacks. He had also worked with Dan Fouts at San Diego. So he had been successful at every stop. Now he'd be going up against a former student of his, Ken Anderson.

The game was played at the Silverdome in Pontiac, Michigan, the first time it hadn't been played in a warm climate. But the domed stadium screened out the ice winds blowing off Lake Michigan. The weather wouldn't be a factor this time. But momentum would.

The Bengals had every chance to grab it, right from

their opening kickoff when 49er Amos Lawrence
fumbled and Cincy recovered at the S.F. 26. But when
Kenny tried to go to Isaac Curtis at the five it was intercepted by Dwight Hicks. A TD there could have
changed the whole game around.

Instead, the 49ers drove 68 yards and scored on a
Montana keeper from the one to take a 7–0 lead. It stayed
that way through the end of the period and in the second
quarter the Bengals drove again. Kenny hit Collinsworth for nineteen yards to the 49ers' nine-yard line,
but Eric Wright stripped the ball from Cris and S.F. had
it again.

After that turnover, Montana led the 49ers on the
longest drive in Super Bowl history, 92 yards, hitting
fullback Earl Cooper from the 11 for the score. It was
14–0 on Ray Wersching's kick and a Wersching field goal
minutes later made it 17–0. Soon after, a fumble of a
squib kick gave S.F. the ball again and another field
goal made it a 20–0 game. By the time momentum began
to swing, it was too late. The 20–0 halftime score was the
biggest margin in a Super Bowl at that point.

But Ken wouldn't quit. He came out in the third period and immediately drove his team 83 yards for their
first score, running it in himself from the five. A 49-yard
pass to Collinsworth highlighted another drive and
brought the ball to the S.F. three yard line. A score now
was crucial. But the 49ers held on a dramatic goal line
stand and got the ball back. That might have been the
biggest turning point.

Still, a fourth-period, 53-yard drive got the Bengals in
again, Kenny hitting Dan Ross from four yards out for
the score. Breech's kick made it 20–14, and the Bengals
were certainly in striking distance.

But a 40-yard field goal by Ray Wersching made it
23–14, and then on another pivotal play, Wright picked
off an Anderson pass and returned it 25 yards, leading
to still another three-pointer and a 26–14 lead. That, in

effect, was the ball game. Cincy scored in the final sixteen seconds, as Ken completed six straight passes in the drive, the final to Ross, making it 26–21. So as they used to say about Bobby Layne, the old Lions and Steeler quarterback, he never lost, time just sometimes ran out on him.

Thus it had run out on Ken Anderson and the Bengals. They had made the costly mistakes and lost the ball game. Ken was 25 of 32 for 300 yards, a gritty performance, but it meant nothing to him because the club lost. There was the usual second-guessing. Some said Ken should have rolled out on fourth down during the 49ers' goal line stand, instead of going to fullback Pete Johnson, which was the expected play.

"That had been our best play in that situation all season," Ken said, "and you go with what got you there."

Ken Anderson was certainly the major factor in getting the Bengals there. The eleven-year pro, on the brink of losing his job in the season's opener, went on to have the greatest season of his career, leading a young team to within a touchdown of its first title.

Like all veteran quarterbacks, Ken has had his ups and downs, seen both the good and the bad part of pro football. He's suffered through injury, played with pain, and taken the anger and frustration of the Cincinnati fans head on. Yet he's endured and prospered, and proved all over again that he's one of the finest quarterbacks in the National Football League.

But as Ken himself said on many occasions, it doesn't mean a thing unless you've won the title. And those who know Ken Anderson, know he won't quit until he gets there.

STATISTICS

Joe Montana

Team	Year	Att.	Comp.	Pct.	Yards	TD	Int.
San Francisco	1979	23	13	56.5	96	1	0
San Francisco	1980	273	176	64.5	1,795	15	9
San Francisco	1981	488	311	63.7	3,565	19	12
NFL Totals		784	500	63.8	5,456	35	21

Danny White

Team	Year	Att.	Comp.	Pct.	Yards	TD	Int.
Dallas	1976	20	13	65.0	213	2	2
Dallas	1977	10	4	40.0	35	0	1
Dallas	1978	34	20	58.8	215	0	1
Dallas	1979	39	19	48.7	267	1	2
Dallas	1980	436	260	59.6	3,287	28	25
Dallas	1981	391	223	57.0	3,098	22	13
NFL Totals		930	539	57.9	7,115	53	44

Joe Theismann

Team	Year	Att.	Comp.	Pct.	Yards	TD	Int.
Washington	1974	11	9	81.8	145	1	0
Washington	1975	22	10	45.5	96	1	3
Washington	1976	163	79	48.5	1,036	8	10
Washington	1977	182	84	46.2	1,097	7	9
Washington	1978	391	187	47.8	2,593	13	18
Washington	1979	395	233	59.0	2,797	20	13
Washington	1980	454	262	57.7	2,962	17	16
Washington	1981	496	293	59.1	3,568	19	20
NFL Totals		2,113	1,157	54.7	14,294	86	89

Ken Anderson

Team	Year	Att.	Comp.	Pct.	Yards	TD	Int.
Cincinnati	1971	131	72	55.0	777	5	4
Cincinnati	1972	301	171	56.8	1,918	7	7
Cincinnati	1973	329	179	54.4	2,428	18	12
Cincinnati	1974	328	213	64.9	2,667	18	10
Cincinnati	1975	377	228	60.5	3,169	21	11
Cincinnati	1976	338	179	53.0	2,367	19	14
Cincinnati	1977	323	166	51.4	2,145	11	11
Cincinnati	1978	319	173	54.2	2,219	10	22
Cincinnati	1979	339	189	55.7	2,340	16	10
Cincinnati	1980	275	166	60.4	1,778	6	13
Cincinnati	1981	479	300	62.6	3,754	29	10
NFL Totals		3,539	2,036	57.5	23,784	160	124